Zeus
Conquering His Heart

I0629481

(Book Two in the Fantastic Immortals Series)

Acknowledgments

I'd like to give a special thank you to **Sadie Sins** for this book's beautiful cover.

Also, thank you to **Christina E. Pilz** for a wonderful beta-read of this novel.

And last but not least, thank you **Della Van Hise** for help with formatting and uploading all my published books. I couldn't do this without you.

When I throw the lightning and summon the thunder, it isn't always out of anger, but from a love so all-consuming it could only be the effect of Eros himself...

Prologue

The harness was made of braided hemp and looped around Zeus's upper thighs and waist. It made an "X" over his back and across his chest. His hips supported most of his weight as he hung from the branches of a large oak tree. The contraption should have chaffed but the pretty nymph who looked after him had swaddled his crotch and buttocks with the softest fleece in the land.

Being a god, he did not soil himself, nor did he suffer pain save boredom, un-met curiosity, and the desire to run free from his incarceration of rope.

Since he was a baby, Zeus had grown up on Earth. For many years he did not know he was different from others in the forest where he was raised, for he rarely met people. Attended to by the nymph Adamanthea, he hung from his harness swing on an old oak for eighteen years, swaying back and forth over the ground he was not allowed to touch. His only playmates were the goats that ran back and forth under his feet, grazing contentedly on the wild nut grass.

At first he cried a lot. Though he did not need food, he enjoyed it, and Adamanthea soothed him with sweet bread and goats' milk, pomegranate juice and tender bites of lamb.

Zeus did not know that the elaborate tangle of hemp that kept him aloft and trapped for years on end might be considered a form of abuse, and though he cried and begged to be let free, he adapted. As a god with untapped powers, his muscles did not atrophy, nor did he suffer much pain.

Adamanthea told him, "The harness is for your own protection because you are such a special boy."

How or why he was "special" was a mystery, but he liked the word. She praised and comforted him and told him funny stories to make him smile. She fed him, bathed him, and gave him toys and puzzles to play with and, later, parchments and story-scrolls to educate him. When Adamanthea deemed he was old enough to understand, she told him more about his origins.

"Your father is a very violent god called a Titan," she began.

Gods were very powerful beings. He'd read about them in the scrolls. He shuddered but longed to hear more.

He learned that his insane Titan father, Cronus, had eaten all his brothers and sisters. This was a horror Zeus could not imagine, and it gave him nightmares and more tears. For weeks after learning the truth of his family, he swung back and forth in the harness in a shocked daze.

Adamanthea told him his mother, Rhea, hid him when he was born and as long as he stayed on Earth but did not touch the ground, he remained invisible to his father's all-seeing eyes. He was safe, protected, but only if he remained aloft, floating on air. Zeus believed Adamanthea's stories, as far-fetched as they were, and fear kept him from running away even when he grew big and strong enough to escape under his own will.

Though he stayed of his own free will, the harness was a cage for him, uncomfortable, biting into his skin when the fleece wore down or he outgrew the straps. His confinement kept him from running, exploring, living free, and he longed for the day when he could leave it.

"When you are fully adult," Adamanthea said, "and you can fend for yourself, you will be released. Then you and your father can face each other as equals. But there will be only one victor."

6

He did not tell her he feared facing his father. How could he be his father's equal? Zeus had no powers of his own.

As he grew older, he began to disbelieve some of her tales. If his parents were gods, then he was a god, too. But he did not feel like a god. For one thing, gods were not helpless. Zeus felt helpless.

Adamanthea was kind to Zeus. She cooked him his favorite foods to eat for fun. He'd come to love stuffed grape leaves, and the wine, cheese and lemon cake she gave him whenever he asked. The wine was strong, on purpose, and Zeus spent much of his life drifting in a kind of ecstatic drunken daze.

The day he learned his godhood did indeed come with powers of life and death, Adamanthea had left the cabin to go down to the river to bathe. Hanging alone, drifting in a dreamy haze, Zeus did not notice the four boys who came into his glade until they were standing all around him, close enough to touch if he swung his legs out.

All the boys had dark hair of varying lengths, and lean brown bodies glistening from the sun's kiss. The two smallest were nude. The other two wore short, white skirts that barely covered anything. All were barefoot.

"Who are you and why are you hanging from this tree?" asked the tallest boy.

"My name is Zeus."

"How old are you?"

"Twelve years."

"Who strung you up?" asked another boy.

"Adamanthea. I think. I'm not sure I remember, maybe my mother—"

"Where are your parents now?" a third asked.

Zeus blinked, his eyes suddenly warm. "Gone." He did not like it that his voice came out hoarse.

"Adamanthea is a sorcerer, you know," the first boy said.

"No, she's a nymph," Zeus corrected.

The boys giggled at his statement.

"Well," said the first, who appeared to be the oldest and the leader, "Adamanthea is not here now. Do you want us to let you down now?"

"No," said Zeus. "I can't touch the ground. I'm not allowed."

"Why?"

"Then I will stop being invisible and my father will find me."

"That makes no sense at all," said the older boy.

Another said, "Do you piss in that harness?"

The littlest smirked and said, "How do you defecate? Does it just drop to the ground? Splat!"

They all laughed except Zeus. Zeus said, "I don't understand. I don't piss or defecate."

"Liar," said the oldest. "Everyone does."

Zeus replied, "I don't."

"That's impossible. But we'll let you down anyway and show you how," the boy said.

"No!" But before Zeus could protest further, the boys grabbed him from all sides, hands gripping his legs, pulling on the ropes, swinging him back and forth. Someone slapped him hard on the buttocks and he swung higher, his face heating, his eyes blurring. The slap came again, followed by giggles.

Zeus barely felt the sting of the blows to his legs and ass, but anger surged through him that left his veins burning. "Stop!"

But they did not stop.

A smoky scent filled him, both pleasurable and strange. A wind came up and the air filled with soft petals and leaves. The forest stretched in a blur of green before him. The river snaked through the woods, out of sight. Adamanthea would not hear him if he called.

All he wanted was for the boys to stop. To leave him alone. To be gone.

The wind whipped his dark hair into his face. He felt the harness loosen. Above all else, whether he believed

8

Adamanthea's stories or not, Zeus instinctively knew it would be cataclysmic to touch the ground.

Zeus felt a prickle of energy move up his spine and into his shoulders. The sensation grew into a heavy pressure and feverish heat that built and built. He held out his arms, hands up. The boys kept laughing, pushing, slapping at him.

Suddenly, a staccato of lightning bolts shot from his hands, relieving the pressure inside him, igniting the air with the muffled sound of thunder and a scent of ozone. He watched as the flames from his fingertips zigzagged into each boy—one, two, three, four—jerking them backward. Eyes wide open, hair standing on end, one by one they dropped to the ground below his feet, still, silent, dead.

Swaying, he stared down at them, their young faces, their lifeless lean bodies all heaped upon the dirt.

Then he began to scream.

Adamanthea came back a short time later, hair filled with flowers, her chiton still wet, and ran to him. She saw the boys on the ground, and then looked up at the weeping Zeus with more sympathy than he'd ever seen from her. "What happened?"

"I don't know. Fire came—" He hiccupped. "—came out of me."

"Yes." Her voice was surprisingly gentle. "This is because you are a god, not human."

"But—but this never happened before."

"Your powers had not yet manifested. They often show at the onset of puberty."

"But I don't understand."

"You're a god," she repeated. "You have power in you to do many things, tricks and magic."

So, she had not lied after all.

"But they're dead. I didn't mean for it to happen."

Adamanthea took his hand in hers and said, "I know you didn't. Don't cry. You have much power, Zeus."

"But I killed them!"

"You have much power. Focus and make them rise. You can do it."

"I—I don't know how."

"Focus." Adamanthea talked in soothing tones, helping him feel his own power and aim it toward the boys, pushing with all his intent to make them live again. More ozone tinged the air. He felt the energy in his spine, the pressure in his shoulders. He pushed it through his arms, pointing his fingers at the little bodies, bidding them to rise. But this time there was no fire, just a pure energy that surrounded him.

One at a time they began to breathe again. Their cheeks pinked. All four boys climbed to their feet and looked about the glade, dazed. Black hair stuck out from their heads, unkempt and brittle as if they had run through a long, hot storm.

Adamanthea stood before them, beautiful, alluring and a little bit frightening. "Go! Leave here at once and do not come back!"

Still shaking, all long limbs and brown skin, the boys ran into the woods silent and skittish as deer.

Adamanthea turned back to Zeus. "There," she said. "None the worse for wear."

From that day on he slowly began to understand what being a god meant. But he had no one but the nymph and the goats to teach him about what that entailed. No one to teach him responsibility for his status and his powers.

Chapter One

The day dawned in fresh pinks and golds and Zeus had just turned eighteen. Upon awakening in his harness, his body swayed in the dew-fresh air. He yawned once, jolting when he thought he heard a sound like a low hum.

Glancing about, he saw six winged strangers appear in the sun-dappled glade. In moments they surrounded him, youthful and naked and reminding him of that long ago day when the little boys threatened to set him free.

For a moment he froze. Then he lifted his hands in front of him, making fists to keep the lightning from coming out of them before he willed it.

The tallest and most beautiful of the strangers stepped closest to Zeus, eyes wide and unafraid. It was as if the stranger saw tall, teenage boys hanging from trees every day.

"We are the Erotes." The tallest one had hair so pale it was almost white. "We are the manifestations of the first of the primordial gods, Eros, twin brother and lover of Chaos from whose union all life began."

Zeus had no idea what that meant. All he could do was stare at these lovely men.

The Erotes were nothing like those boys from his past who had tormented him. For one thing, they had wings, some feathered, others flat and multicolored like moth wings. They had golden skin and blond hair. And they all had green-gold eyes that flashed like sparks from a winter hearth.

"What is a primordial god?" Zeus asked.

"The gods who came from the void, unborn yet living. Flesh and blood transmogrified from the nothing."

"Are there many?"

"There are four. Chaos and Eros are the first two primordials, and then came Gaia and Tartarus," the tall, winged man answered.

"Why have you come here to me?"

"We always do Eros's bidding."

"But why would he bid you to come here? I don't know anyone called Eros. How is it he knows me?"

"You are known to many, Zeus. Soon you will understand."

Zeus thought about that. He was a god, yes, and his father seemed to be famous. Maybe it was all about that. "Are you here to help me fight my father?"

The speaker nodded. "Yes, and so much more."

"Oh, thank you. Thank you so much!" He was so excited at the prospect of being freed he almost could not find his voice. A heat began to form behind his eyes.

Adamanthea came out of her hut, a frown creasing her normally smooth features. She crossed her arms and nodded toward Zeus. "It is your eighteenth birthday today. I see the Erotes have come for you, Zeus."

"You knew they were coming?" he asked.

"Yes. You're a man now. No longer a child. You must go outward, into all the worlds, and find your destiny as a god."

"You are coming, too," Zeus said. It was not a question.

"No. My place is here. I'm an Earth spirit. But you need to go with these lovely men. They can teach you what I cannot. They can make you strong and free from your father's wrath. Trust them, sweetheart. Go with my love. I will never forget you."

As he heard her words, tears splashed down his face. She was the only mother, the only comfort he had ever known. "But I don't want to leave you."

"You will be fine. All fledglings leave their nests eventually. I have taught you this. And you have learned it by observing the birds in the forest that have surrounded you your whole life."

He pressed his lips tight, trying to breathe.

Adamanthea came up to him and placed her hand on his damp face, caressing. "I won't forget you, Zeus. Not ever."

"I won't forget you, either." His voice shook.

The tall Erotes began to undo his harness. For a moment he ignored them all, staring only at Adamanthea until she slipped out of his sight behind him.

Turning his attention toward the golden men, he realized something truly amazing was happening. He was being freed. He was going to touch ground for the first time ever. It felt strange and exhilarating at once.

When his feet finally hit the ground, his knees trembled, barely holding him. For that moment he looked down at his freed body, so tall now, his dark hair brushing in long waves against his shoulders and chest. He was at last grown man. He knew he had to go with these strange men or he would never be safe from Cronus. He knew so little about being a god and he was all-too hungry to learn.

Slowly, he fell to his hands, palms out, fingers grasping earth and weed. He began to sob uncontrollably. He turned on his knees and reached instinctively for Adamanthea, but she coldly stepped away. Still, he could see the tears streaming down her apple cheeks.

The Erotes surrounded him, hands on his shoulders and arms. He felt the breeze of their wings as they lightly flapped. A feather brushed his naked back. He felt grateful for their presence, but so weak. Surely, he could never fight someone as strong as a Titan in this state. He had no hope of escaping his father's insane appetite and was convinced he would be eaten just as his brothers and sisters had been.

He might be a god, but he was a god who could barely even stand.

He looked up at the six Erotes through his tears. "I can't fight. I don't know how. You seem limitless in your powers. Why can't you fight my father for me? Why do I have to be the one?"

The speaker knelt in front of Zeus and placed both hands alongside his head, tilting it up until they were face to face.

"We each have power but it is limited, and we are based only on pure love and eroticism. We are not fighters. But you, Zeus, your power is magnificent and unlimited. You have some time. You will not see your father right away. Eros will teach you. We will teach you. You have great and boundless energy. You are the only one who can fight him and win. We will teach you mastery over your body. Eros himself can teach you about your mind and your god powers, and finally, how to fight in all ways."

Zeus shook his head. The words sounded good, but he did not feel powerful at all. "If everything about Cronus is true, he is coming for me this moment. He has known where I am as soon as my hands and feet touched the earth."

The winged man leaned closer, his lips almost touching Zeus's. "Shh, my beauty. You have time. We are bringing you to Eros's abode in the sky. It will take Cronus some time to locate it. You will be safe for now." He stood, taking Zeus's hands in his.

The other five Erotes grasped Zeus by the arms and legs and flew him up into the dawn. In a short time, he rose past fluffy clouds and into the burnt orange, early morning sky. They went fast. So fast that Zeus became dizzy.

A floating landscape with a large house suddenly appeared before them, white and gleaming with pillars that looked carved from fire, and golden-pink windows that flashed a brightness so great it stung the eyes. Zeus gasped at the beauty.

They entered through a great, arched doorway, and finally the Erotes set Zeus down.

He managed to stand on his own for the first time, shivering, shaking, though it only took seconds before he felt strong enough to walk his first steps. As he put each foot forward, his confidence strengthened. After only five steps, he walked as if he had already known how his whole life.

14

He heard whispers behind him. "He is strong." "He has a fine will." "Magnificent." "The rumors do not do him justice."

He ignored the winged beings for the moment, fascinated by all he faced. He could see endless rooms of jeweled hearths and magic candlelight and sofas made of downy foam. Pink and white roses burst forth from the walls as if at random.

The six Erotes surrounded him, each man majestic in splendor as the grandest of dreams. The tallest one who had, so far, answered all of Zeus's questions, sported golden wings like a moth's, each diaphanous panel patterned with a dark spot in the center. He faced Zeus.

"Welcome to Eros's abode," he said. "My name is Anteros. For now, I am in charge." He wore nothing, and his lean-muscled body glowed the color of golden sunlight. Zeus could not stop looking at him.

"Eros is appalled at the abuse you have suffered," Anteros continued. "He apologizes that he cannot be here himself until later."

"I have not been abused," Zeus countered. "Adamanthea was very good to me."

"No child, most especially a god, should ever be raised in a harness. Eros has made it an order that we will see you treated with the finest of luxuries until he arrives."

"And he will teach me about my powers?"

Anteros nodded. "Among many things. We have a short time before your father locates you, months, maybe only weeks," Anteros said. "In that time, you will learn all you need to know."

"But what if I don't want to do battle? What if I just want to go back to my harness?" In such a strange place, like nothing he had ever imagined, he began to be panicky and unsure. Adamanthea had said there would only be one victor. What if his father won and ate him? The known reality of the harness seemed not such a bad thing compared to that.

"You have not been given that choice." Anteros handed Zeus a golden chalice as if he had manifested it from the air. "Now. Drink."

Zeus drank the wine of the moth-winged gods. Jewelweed and thorn. Sweet Olympian rain. Warm tongue and lip. His tears dried. A sensation of vibrancy, like a fresh spring wind, moved through his muscles and veins. It was as if he breathed the sweetness of rivers and starlight and blooming lilies all at once.

He held out the empty chalice. "May I have more, please?"

Smiling, Anteros went to a high table, took a pitcher in hand and re-filled the chalice.

It was the sweetest concoction Zeus had ever tasted. He could not get enough. The chalice he drank from was pure gold, carved with winged youths facing outward in a circle, hands clasped. The carvings were the exact likenesses of the beautiful men who now stood before him.

His body thrummed to the honeyed flavor and scent, and tingled from its effects. "What is it?"

"Ambrosia. You are already immortal, but this keeps you young, and gives you strength to focus for the ages."

The winged youths forced him to drink more and more of the sweet ambrosia until he was full to bursting. Zeus did not rebel. He felt thirstier than he could ever remember being.

After they said he had had enough, they escorted him to the baths.

Zeus had only ever been bathed by Adamanthea. She used oil and a dull, wooden wedge to scrape his skin, then wet cloths to wipe the dust and sweat and tears from his body. He had never actually seen a bathing room, let alone had an actual bath.

The bath of Eros's abode consisted of a huge room flanked by marble fountains in the shapes of leaping dolphins, lounging mermaids and mermen, and whales spouting glistening founts of blue-tinged liquid. In the center of the room

16

a large pool glistened, with stairs carved into the sides leading down to the clear depths. Zeus could see the pool bottom tiles had been designed in a mosaic of two mermen and two mermaids intertwined.

The room smelled damp but fresh, like spring dew at dawn. Within that air he also detected scents of lavender, sandalwood, and sweet pine. Light wavered from an unseen source, and held a soft, rosy glow.

Zeus expected the Erotes to oil him and scrape away the dust, but instead Anteros led him to a small enclosure. He tugged the swaddle cloth from Zeus's hips, and then gently pushed him forward. Three spigots emerged from the wall and sprayed warm water, dousing him. He yelped in surprise.

Anteros said, "Rinse yourself clean here and you can soak with us in the warm waters of the main pool."

The water sluiced over him and the sensation of it hitting his skin was so good Zeus could only gasp. He'd endured storms and rain and drizzle his whole life, weather pattering him at random, but nothing like this gentle waterfall of controlled power.

When his skin and hair were soaked, he emerged from the open stall and saw a spectacle before him. All six Erotes were floating or playing in various parts of the large pool. Their hair and wings dripped as they leapt and swam.

Zeus thought the more delicate butterfly and moth wings might wilt under the pressure of the liquid, but those wings remained rigid and when they turned in the water, behaved like fins. The two with feathered wings dove about the water's surface, making waves. Their wings looked impervious to liquid, the water beading and sliding away each time they emerged to the air.

These Erotes were fantastic swimmers. Also, Zeus could not help but observe how their young bodies gleamed in the sheen of dampness. With hard chests, sculpted buttocks and perpetually half-hard penises, they drew the eye. It was difficult not to stare, or to feel another kind of heat in his veins separate from the ambrosia.

Anteros came up the pool's white steps to greet him as Zeus approached, gazing at him up and down. "You are a fine specimen."

Zeus looked down at his own darker body. He was the only one here with black hair and eyes, and deeply sun-browned skin. But he could see, as if for the first time, that he was no longer a child. His body had grown long and well-muscled despite no exercise his whole life. He was a god, just as the Erotes were, and extreme beauty was a god-trait whether or not the god grew up in a harness.

"Come into the water," Anteros said. "It is warm and sweet."

Zeus smelled lavender, light and soothing. His pleasure as he entered the water was so great he almost began to weep.

Anteros, sensing his emotions, soothed him with soft words and soft palms pressed to his cheeks. "Everything is a shock to you right now," he said quietly. "But you are well. And we will help you. You have many supporters, and friends you have not yet met."

Anteros made more soothing sounds and kissed him on the forehead and on both cheeks. "Now, now, try to relax."

Anteros was the most beautiful man Zeus had ever seen, with a stronger glow than the other Erotes, a firm, chiseled jaw line, and wide-set eyes. His silvery white hair hung in glowing ribbons that drifted to damp points upon his shoulders. His hands were smooth as flower petals, his wings like a magnificent, diaphanous cloak.

Gentle Anteros allowed Zeus to clutch at his hands, lean into his arms and breathe deeply of him as he rested in the silken waters. More chalices appeared with more ambrosia. Zeus was encouraged to drink until drunk.

The heat in his veins kept pounding, receding, and then pounding again. He watched the naked cupids play. He stared as they wrapped their bodies around each other and undulated, their faces filled with bliss. Zeus had never seen anything like this.

Only Anteros did not play, staying by Zeus's side, keeping a strong arm about his shoulders.

Zeus wondered if he would ever feel free like those five leaping, happy men, if he might ever feel the energy these youthful-looking gods embodied. At the moment he was so overwhelmed, tired, and dazed on ambrosia that he could not think. He continued to worry about his father finding him.

They all stayed in the pool for quite some time. Zeus found himself nodding into a doze, only to be lightly shaken by Anteros's grip. "Wake, young one. Let's dry off and find you a place to rest."

Later, it was Anteros who showed Zeus to a sumptuous white bed in a dim room with windows dotted with starlight. He left him there. Zeus did not want him to leave, but was too overwhelmed to call him back.

Zeus had never slept in a bed before. It was magnificent, soft and pillowed, cupping his body in all the right places.

Despite the luxury, at first he could not relax. He wished Anteros was there to talk to him, comfort him as he had done in the pool. Everything was so strange. Finally, he succumbed to the effects of the ambrosia combined with the shock and exhaustion of his new surroundings, and dreamed of feathers, moth wings, and clouds.

Chapter Two

When Zeus woke, starlight still rained against the smooth windows of the bedroom. He thought it must still be night and tried to sleep again, but failed.

He got up and wandered in the shadows of the room, exploring. A table of polished wood stood in the center of the room. On it were stacks of thin sheets of parchment connected with unseen binding, along with some strange devices that looked like empty, black windows. He touched them and felt their alien coldness. They remained hollow to him, mysterious.

He wandered to a wall of shelves, touching the objects there: glass statues of fauns, an onyx ball the size of his head, more bound parchments. The starlight was enough to see by, and brought out all the details. He found a chest of drawers and inside them discovered wraps, chitons, and carefully folded cloaks. Though the Erotes wore no clothes, Zeus felt uncomfortable unswaddled, and chose a shimmering, silver wrap to tie about his waist.

Still un-used to being mobile, Zeus was hesitant to leave the room. But he was restless. He went to the door, which automatically swung open before him as if sensing his presence. A long, white hallway stretched to unseen rooms. He remembered Anteros leading him down that hall to his bed, but not much more about the house. He'd been tired, still overwhelmed by his change of venue, and groggy from the ambrosia.

Now he wanted to explore. But he was afraid.

Yes, he was a god. He had powers. But he still didn't understand what that meant. And his father was still out there, still hunting him. How long did he have before he was forced to confront him and possibly be imprisoned for life in a giant Titan stomach? Immortals could not die. What might that mean, being kept in a dark, airless pit like that for years? Were his brothers and sisters even conscious, suffering? He pictured his father as a monster and could not rid the thought from his mind.

He shuddered, and forced himself to take a step forward into the brightness that was Eros's abode. He stopped after two steps, listening for sounds of life. He heard only silence, like a soft wind, which did nothing to bolster his confidence. There was a slight scent of asphodel in the air, faintly sweet. The air wafted cool over his arms, chest and legs.

He took more hesitant steps, and slowly reached out to touch one wall. It felt smooth, cold to the touch. Dry. Unnatural. For a moment he grew dizzy. He thought of Adamanthea, her soothing touches. Trees and rain and the textures and scents of home. His eyesight wavered in sudden warmth.

Certainly, he did not miss his leather and hemp harness, or the sheep's wool padding to keep the straps from chafing his legs, back and shoulders. But he did miss Adamanthea. All he had ever known was that little glade. He knew every leaf of grass, every goat's name, every tree within his sight and how they spoke in their voices of airy growth. The routine of his life, though boring to the point of agony, had comforted him.

His tongue craved her lemon cake. His body yearned for her consoling touch. He did not ever call her *mother* but he had thought it.

He had been stuck his whole life, unmoving. He had been given a role and could not un-do it. Nothing had ever been his choice alone. But he was a man now. A god. Surely he could make his own choices. But the barrier of his insane father stood before him. He was not safe.

His hand shook as he raised it to his face, feeling his own grief. His lungs seemed frozen in this moment. He could not manage a deep breath.

"You're an innocent," said a tranquil, low voice behind him.

Zeus turned, expecting one of the Erotes. Instead, he saw a tall man in a sweeping green robe that looked as if it emanated light from within. Curving from the back of the robe were giant wings, greater than those of the Erotes, and white enough to make Zeus squint.

"What?" Zeus tried to breathe in again but found himself still in a state of shock, his muscles tight, his body like a separate entity, a cage of skin that was all of a sudden uncomfortable, betraying its heavy emotions, its homesickness, its state of feeling lost.

"Baby gods are so fragile." The winged man took a step forward, extending his right hand, palm up. "My name is Eros. Welcome to my home."

Zeus could only stare. He'd never seen anyone more beautiful, not even Adamanthea. Eros had silvery blond hair like sunlight, and eyes the color of new spring leaves. His skin, lighter than Zeus's, looked as if it had been polished in pale bronze paint.

So this was Eros, the primordial god Anteros had told him of. Something inside Zeus fluttered and came to life as he stared at him. He could not help but be drawn to this light, and felt a strange, arousing heat.

Eros did not seem fazed by Zeus's shock. Instead, he tilted his head and gave a soft smile. "This will be hard for you at first, I know. But come." He held out his hand again. "Has anyone given you a tour of the house?"

Zeus looked at the outstretched hand. Was he to take it? To follow?

"Don't be afraid." Eros tone was like a caress. "You are young and your tears will dry. No one will ever hurt you in my home. You are safe."

"But they said my father—"

"Ah, yes. Cronus is a problem. And soon he may come to knock down these walls if we don't take matters into our own hands at first. But we have time. And when you are ready, I will prefer it if you go to him and not bring him here."

Zeus blinked back more warmth. "You—you're not going to protect me?"

"Better." Eros brought his hand to Zeus's, which still hung limp at his side. He clasped it, palm to palm. "I will teach you to protect yourself. Come." He gave a light tug. "Let me show you the arboretum."

Zeus nodded, mainly because he did not know what else to do, and followed Eros down the long corridor. The god's wings were so big they brushed like branches of silk against his shoulder. The hand in his was warm and strong. Zeus's skin prickled with a sort of coldness that turned to fever, and he wondered what his hand felt like in return.

After a moment, the touch of their hands became something more. As they walked, a tingle shot up Zeus's arm. His whole body became suffused with a sudden lightness of being, of sun-warmth. The word 'serenity' came to him. And resilience. Supremacy. Ardor.

Eros said something that sounded garbled, but Zeus's mind instantly translated it to mean, "As a god you will learn quickly. Science. Philosophy. Your brain can translate any language you hear, such as in this moment as I speak Novoxian, a language more ancient than Sanskrit and very difficult to learn."

"I understood that," Zeus whispered.

"And now you need only hear it once for your mind to open and accept it in fluency. Speak to me now in Novoxian, Zeus."

Zeus focused a moment, thought about the sound of Eros's words, and let them flow through his thoughts. He chose some at random. "Tree. Goat. Nymph."

"Excellent." Eros turned toward him. "You can speak full sentences now. Once you hear a language, it will never leave you."

Already, Zeus was amazed. He squeezed Eros's hand, which squeezed back, and the lightness within him increased. He suddenly had a thousand questions brimming like a tide in his mind. His lips quivered, but he gave Eros only a shaky smile.

He decided he liked it here in Eros's home very much. And Eros as well. A new yearning filled his heart.

Zeus realized, as they walked, this house somewhere in the sky was much bigger than he had thought. The halls seemed endless. They passed by open rooms with statues, furniture, beds, fountains, but turned into none of them.

Finally, they reached a giant archway that looked as if it were formed of blue and white marble. On the curved arch were elaborate carvings of trees, their branches and leaves entwined in complex knots.

Zeus's head tilted back, taking it all in.

"It's a mix of lapis and crystal," Eros said.

Zeus knew his gemstones well. Stuck in his harness, he'd had a lot of time to read the scrolls and parchments Adamanthea brought to him, and she had verbally taught him lessons of everything she could think of.

"It's beautiful," Zeus said. The word, however, seemed inadequate for what he was looking at.

"Yes, it is amazing what can be accomplished when an intelligent being sets their mind to it."

Before they crossed the threshold, Zeus could already hear the sounds of moving water, humming wind, chattering life. The arboretum bloomed before them.

For a moment, Zeus thought he'd been transported back home to Adamanthea's cute little cottage and the tree branch he'd called home. A different sort of light than that in the hallway, with a more yellow cast, sparked the leaves of a hundred trees, and caught itself in the laps and waves of a tiny, glistening brook. A wooden bridge with ornate, red handrails crossed the brook to a sun-speared glen beyond it where birds played, and little lavender flowers bloomed.

When Zeus looked up, he saw a great, latticed dome. Between the latticework were windows that showed a thousand winking stars. He could barely take in all that he was seeing.

24

"But where does the light come from?" he heard himself ask.

"This place manufactures ambient light through a holographic illusion."

That was a language Zeus did not yet speak. But he did understand the word *illusion*.

"You mean none of this is real?"

"It's all real. The light is stirred in mechanically, without a visible source. It's better than marring the scene with a thousand lanterns, don't you think?"

Zeus didn't know what to think, but he nodded. "Did you build this?"

Eros smiled. "All of it. Yes."

"You're an artist?"

"Aren't we all?"

"I don't know."

"Everyone, even mortals, creates. Home, children, tools, stories, songs, sculptures, new ways of looking at things, doing things—all go, in their millions of parts, to make up a world, small or large. Vast empires or houses for dolls. It's all co-created."

Blinking in the false sunlight, standing on soft grass, Zeus suddenly had more questions than he could hold onto in his thoughts. What was Eros, exactly? Where did he come from? Zeus was a god. But Eros was a primordial god. What did that even mean?

As if reading his mind, Eros lifted his hand from Zeus's grip and held it up.

"You have much to learn, Zeus. All in good time. I am here for you. I brought you here first because I wanted to show you something from the heart. A foundation to get you started. Never forget that at the core of everything is simply this: life. It exists because it can. It is an effort to put forth all possibility with the best creative force it can."

"It?"

"Life itself. The force that makes us exist. The energy of all existence. It is a diamond that lives in every scrap of matter waiting for its moment to shine. In all you will learn here, and on into the future, never forget that diamond that waits to reveal its splendor. It is all around you all the time, even in darkness, even in despair."

Zeus liked the words, but didn't quite feel them sink in. "But why me? Why have you, personally, come to teach me? What am I to you?"

"While falling between the days and hours where I spend much of my existence, I have seen visions of you. Your power. Zeus, you have been known to me since the day you were born."

"But you could not help me then."

"No one could find you. When your talents began to show, I felt you. It was then I decided to bring you here when you were ready."

Zeus didn't know what to think about that. Here was a man with a lot of power, a lot of claims. And a beauty that was more than distracting. For all the allure of the arboretum in the stars, Eros was the centerpiece. Again Zeus's eyes were drawn to the gleaming feathered wings, the strong face, and the green burn of the eyes. The ends of Eros's silver-gold hair slid along his shoulders and mixed with the feathers along his back where the gown split to make room for the wings.

This immortal god said he would teach Zeus. But in truth he shattered Zeus's mind, blinding him. Next to Eros, Zeus felt like a shadow just beginning to find his way. Still a boy.

The leaves on the trees shuddered. The stars flickered through the latticework of the dome. Eros radiated limitless allure and possibility.

Zeus took a deep breath, his lungs still quivering, and said, "I want to start learning right away."

*

The house was filled with many rooms, more than Zeus could explore in a day. After the arboretum, one of the first rooms Eros took him to held a large dirt arena, with walls of weapons, knives, swords, arrows, and other items Zeus could not identify.

"You are a god of storms," Eros said. "You can make lightning and throw thunderbolts so you won't have much need of weapons. But it is good to know the skill of swordplay, wrestling, and knife work. And the bow is quite the art form. It is a challenge. And for immortals, we need challenge. We need entertainment."

"I killed four boys once," Zeus said.

"Knowing how to kill and how not to kill is a lesson we can work on."

"It didn't matter. I raised them back to life anyway."

Zeus expected Eros to be impressed. Instead, the golden eyebrows narrowed.

"Do not think you can be crass about that." He spoke gently, but Zeus felt mortified. "You took something from them. Every death is a loss, like an obliteration of an entire universe. The seconds or minutes they missed? Do not discount their importance. There is now a notch in each of their minds that can never be healed."

Zeus swallowed hard against tenseness in his throat. His eyes blurred. "I did not know. "

"I realize that. And you did not know how to control your power. But you will learn."

"Why are there mortals in the first place? It's a horror. Death is wrong."

"Yes. But you will come to understand there are all possibilities in an environment that contains infinity. All good and all bad. Everything that can ever be. The myth of the soul gives mortals some hope that they are, in fact, immortal."

"The myth of the soul?"

"Even I, who came from the nothing, do not have a full understanding of everything. The soul is one of those mysteries

I still pursue. I have experienced much that tells me it may exist. I have much more to experience to confirm my hope."

Zeus did not know how to respond to that. Instead, he embraced the sword.

For his first lesson, Zeus learned how to hold a sword, how to raise it, how to stand and balance. He was given a series of movements to memorize and practice. He learned quickly, and felt an eagerness for more.

Soon he was sparring with Eros, kicking up a lot of dirt, making a lot of mistakes, but still amazed at what he could do. Eros could not be beaten, and Zeus did not even try. The god was too quick, and his wings stretched out on either side of his body, making him even more imposing than ever. But Zeus picked up the moves quickly, and his god-mind woke to new things like a flower opening to drink light and dew.

Like foreign languages, the techniques for swordplay were already inside him waiting for the proper stimulus to flood his mind with knowledge. Every time Eros taught him a move, ten more moves drew themselves in pictures across his thoughts.

"Leaps and bounds," Eros muttered.

"What?" Zeus, breathing hard, laid his sword aside.

"It is a delight to introduce you to the wonders of being a god."

Such a short time ago, he had been in tears. Now Zeus was smiling. "What's next?"

Chapter Three

Ambrosia filled him so that he was never hungry. Still, he craved the elixir all the time. All the different textures and colors Eros offered him were equally delightful. Red and sweet. Smoky orange. Violet with an edge of salt.

The drink gave him a drunken feeling, but different from the wine Adamanthea had served him to keep him quiet in his more despairing moments in the harness. Ambrosia came with a luscious spread through his veins, as if he were in more control, not less, as if his power swelled. And it gave Zeus voluptuous dreams.

If he drank too much, it did also act like wine. When drunk on ambrosia, he had trouble standing, walking, talking. But in the right amounts, he brimmed with a quivering ecstasy unlike anything he'd ever experienced.

The first night he'd spent in the home of Eros, Zeus had been in shock, and his sleep had been skittery and dark and restless. But after he and Eros trained with the sword, his second night of sleep came with billowing peach skies, and himself floating upon them. He swam in liquid gold seas while yellow cake moons rose and set above him. His body tingled in pleasure. His cock, which he had not much use for his whole life, swelled to a thick hardness that gave him a sense of wonder, abandon, yearning. He wanted something he could not name. This nameless thing came with building pleasure, but did not seem complete.

He woke aroused, but excited to seek more lessons, so ignored the bobbing protrusion at his middle. He tied on his silver sash, looping it tightly between his legs and pulling his cock down and back so that it was forced to curve against his balls. He didn't know why he wanted to hide it, but he wasn't ready to admit to Eros that a private part of his body was out of control. Though the Erotes never hid their bodies or their hard cocks, Zeus was not ready to reveal his.

His cheeks heated as he thought of how Eros might look at him, of what he might say.

Eros greeted him in the main pool room. Three of the Erotes were swimming, naked and alluring. Zeus looked upon them with a breathlessness he tried to hide. The reflections of splashing water glimmered in Eros's bright eyes as he watched his winged companions.

Not turning away from the view, Eros asked, "Back to the sparring room?"

"Yes" Zeus said, eager for more information.

Picking up two flasks of ambrosia to sip en route, Eros led the way. When they got there, Eros began undoing his green robe.

Zeus saw Eros's hard-muscled chest, lean and bronze, as the edges of the robe slipped from his shoulders, catching on his wings. Zeus had the strongest response to him, his bound cock twitching and veins burning, but lowered his gaze. Curious, and in an attempt to distract himself, he asked, "What is the next lesson?"

"Wrestling. It is done in the nude."

Backing up one step, Zeus shook his head. "I—I was hoping for archery. I wanted to try it."

Eros let go of his robe. It hung against his wings where they attached at his spine, the front open all the way down to his abdomen.

Zeus swallowed hard at the lovely sight, skin hairless and silken, no navel, muscles taut at the ribs and stomach, the lovely dents at the hips.

Eros's eyes were soft. His facial expression showed not a hint of judgment. "I understand. You are young. But even boys learn the art of wrestling at a young age."

Zeus blinked, turning away from the beautiful god. "I—I just don't want to do that right now."

"Archery it is, then. For today. Come with me."

Zeus felt a hand on his arm. He flinched for a moment, but went willingly. Eros was so kind. He could not imagine the god would willingly judge or hurt him, but Zeus did not want to be a disappointment so early on. He did not want Eros examining him, or ever telling him something was wrong or different about him because he could not control an erection that the Erotes seemed to so proudly display at all times.

This was different for Zeus. Personal. He'd never experienced anything like this. He did not want to be playful about it. Or dismissive. The thought left him hollow. Even a little angry.

For archery, Eros had set up a separate room that felt like the outdoors, like the arboretum, with trees and plants growing through a hard floor, and circular targets positioned at random with small, bull's-eye centers. On the side walls roses bloomed, real-looking, three-dimensional, ivory and red.

As Eros took up the bow and cocked the arrow, the fluidity of his movement mesmerized Zeus. It looked so natural for him. Eros aimed and hit the bulls-eye first try.

Zeus could not look away. The sleeve of Eros's robe had fallen back; his bicep was rounded, the sinews on his hard arms stood out. He took another arrow from his quiver and it was like watching a graceful dance. Eros stepped forward, balanced up. His wings fluffed. His hair fell in a curve against his forehead, gold on gold. The arrow went flying as if with a life of its own, seeking touch, penetration, and completion.

Zeus felt caught in a dream.

"Would you like to try now?" Eros held out the bow, a finely crafted piece, taut but lightweight.

"Have you ever shot a person?" asked Zeus.

"Only those I love." Eros raised one eyebrow and smiled.

Zeus frowned. "That's not—"

"Go ahead. Try for the target. Here's an arrow. Hold it like this." Eros moved up close to Zeus, emanating a summery heat, positioning the weapon in his hands.

Zeus backed up a step. Dizzy. "I don't feel right."

His body began to shake. He couldn't see. He felt Eros lift his left arm, hold it out, and the touch obliterated all thought. He felt power surge through him, up and out. He heard a crash. Then another. The heat in his body felt fiery. His fingertips burned.

Another crash. He opened his eyes, saw the trail of the lightning just disappearing, and the target on the tree trunk that Eros had shot at was blackened, half-melted. Another black scar, the length of two arrows, marred one of the rose-enhanced walls.

Eros's hands caressed Zeus's forehead, as if to sweep away the faint ache within that was just beginning.

"Control of your power," he said. "I will teach you that, too."

That was when Zeus realized that, without his will, the lightning had come from him again. Uncontrolled. Unwanted.

A strange rage well up in Zeus. A fire burned behind his eyes.

"No! I can't do it!" It seemed to come from nowhere and everywhere, this instant frustration, a mad, blind fury. He pushed the soft hand away from his face, realize his chest was heaving. He didn't know where to be or stand, how to breathe anymore, how to even speak. In a tumultuous whirl of perception, Zeus ran from the room.

*

The bedroom was lit only by starlight. The shadows lay still. Darkness never faltered, never disappointed.

Zeus could breathe again, feel his body, his muscles, his blood, air in his lungs. His thoughts calmed. Clarified.

He lay back and the coolness of the sheets sent him back to the glade, his tree, the safety of his harness and his youth. He could almost smell the shaded woods, the freshness of the out-of-sight brook that sang to him since he was a baby. The weedy nut-grasses bloomed their white-honey flowers on the air.

His skin itched a little. He still felt hot, but less so, the crazy fever abating. He closed his eyes and dozed for a moment. A gray peace surrounded him.

He felt the air swirl against his arms and chest, sensed slow movement, heard a step. The edge of his bed dented. He opened his eyes.

Anteros knelt before him, naked and lovely, his moth wings shimmering like sheets of mica behind him. His nakedness seemed effortless. He was aroused, as usual, proud and unconcerned. Zeus thought he could never ever feel that way, that free, so completely open and vulnerable. He would die of it, he was sure, his immortality a slap in the face.

He looked away from the stunning Erotes and said, "Eros sent you."

"Not exactly." Anteros settled himself in the bed, sitting against a pillow beside the reclining Zeus, his wings folded tight against his back. "Eros is linked to all of six of us. We are his manifestations."

"You're not alive, then?" Zeus asked.

"Oh, we're very much alive. Manifestations are like tulpas, and take on lives of their own after a time. We are here through our own free will now, living in this mansion, free to love each other. We are happy."

"So does a link with him mean you feel everything he feels?"

"On some level, yes," Anteros answered. "Sometimes we can even see through each others' eyes, but not always. It depends upon our moods, our focus, or whether we wish to close each other out. We have that freedom, too, to be separate and isolated when we need space."

"I wanted that space today… awhile ago, I guess. I couldn't see or think."

"I understand."

"I am feeling so many things all at once," Zeus confessed. "The lightning came out of my hands again, in a way I had no hope to control."

"Zeus, you have been here only two days. You lived in a harness your whole life. Give yourself time."

"I am a god. I should have learned everything there is to know in two days."

Anteros laughed softly. For a moment, Zeus thought maybe he was laughing at him, but the sound was too soothing for that to be true. Nothing but affection radiated from this man. In the bedroom, in the starlight, no threat existed.

"Do not be hard on yourself," Anteros said. "No one here expects you to be anyone but who you are."

"That's untrue."

"How?"

"I'm a god. There are expectations from that. I have been noticed and targeted by a primordial god. What does that mean? And I am expected to fight my violent father, a god in his own right with far more power than I. Those expectations are only the beginning." He wondered if he sounded petulant. But he was only missing home. Missing his innocence. He did not even really know why. This place was far better than hanging in a harness all day, despite Adamanthea's tender compassion and care.

Out the corner of his eye, Zeus saw Anteros nod, eyelashes sweeping down to shadow his perfect, dimpled cheeks. "Hmm, I see. You are right, of course. It is a lot to embrace at once. I will tell you, Zeus, here in this place we are insulated, spoiled. We follow orders, whatever Eros wants, but we are not all that adept at dealing with people who know nothing of our ways, and I would say we were perhaps a bit clumsy and insensitive in introducing you to it all. I will take the blame, of course. I was in charge of this mission."

"I don't blame you for my misgivings and weaknesses," Zeus said.

"Zeus, you are not weak. Never believe that!"

"I am. What happened today, the lightning—"

"That's not weakness. That's just strength manifesting, ever greater and more powerful. You are learning. How can that be a bad thing? But patience is a lesson, too, and now you are learning about that. How to listen to yourself, feel yourself, be yourself."

Zeus turned his head away, air expelling hard from this throat. "This morning I couldn't even control my body." His teeth gritted as his voice lowered. "I had to wrap the scarf tighter—" He stopped.

"Young one, there are ways to control that as well. Or not. It is all up to you. But if you want relief you may ask any of us for help. Or you can just touch yourself like this." Anteros reached down and gripped his proud cock in his fist, pulling up.

Immediately, Zeus's face heated. "Anteros! Don't do that!" He moved away on the bed, his back facing Anteros, his legs hanging off the edge. Again, he was poised to flee.

"Why ever not?" Anteros asked.

"Just—I don't know. I don't know! It's Eros. His proximity or something. The way he says things, like when he said he shoots only those he loves. And then when he touched me while teaching me the bow and arrow… it made me feel strange."

He could hear the smile in Anteros's voice now. "Everyone falls in love with Eros. He should be more circumspect about that, more sensitive. Sometimes he is. Sometimes he just has to be reminded."

Zeus turned on the bed, pulling one knee up, facing Anteros again. "Really? Everyone? That makes it far, far worse! And the fact that Eros might not pay attention to that, or care--" He let out a quick breath. "I should leave here. Search for another teacher."

"But where would you go?"

Zeus stared at the bedspread, a deep purple cloth that ran to dark pinks in the errant wrinkles that glistened in the starlight.

"Zeus." Anteros was almost whispering. "You must stay here. I promise you we'll all be more sensitive to you. I promise."

"I don't want you to change your behavior for me."

"All right. But know this. We've all already grown to love you."

He winced. Pressed his lips together hard. Finally, he looked up at Anteros's gentle face. "I don't know what that means."

"Another lesson, then. Love. That's a hard one. You have little foundation for it."

"Adamanthea loved me."

"In her way. But you were not raised among groups of people, or among gods. It's all new for you. People. Socializing. Friendship."

"The goats were my friends."

Anteros let out a short laugh. "I love goats. They are wonderful creatures!"

The edges of Zeus's mouth curved in the beginning of a smile. For awhile they sat in mutual, comforting silence.

Finally, Anteros said, "Feeling a little better?"

"Yes."

Anteros reached out and took his hand. "Come. Let's go to the pool, drink ambrosia until we can't stand up."

The temptation was too much, and really, he didn't want to leave this place, or find another teacher. While Zeus was aware the ambrosia contributed to his heat, he could not resist. He followed Anteros to the fountain room.

Chapter Four

Though there was manifested ambient light everywhere, the fountain room—or pool room as they called it—held pink and gold pulsating lanterns with clear windows that glowed. Roses bloomed from the walls, along with decorative fountains depicting dolphins, mermen, and conch shells spouting luminous water.

Zeus lay back in the main pool, half-floating, listening to the patter of liquid hitting liquid, how it echoed like endless rain, how it chattered to itself, calming him.

He had already drunk three—or was it four—chalices of ambrosia. The red kind that tasted of oranges and honey. It was his favorite. In the background, he was also overhearing snippets of conversation.

For most of the day, Eros had stayed away. But now he was close.

Zeus had not even had to turn his head and look to know he'd entered the glinting room. The very atmosphere went from light to cloying. The air became slippery, tinged with a sweetness he could not define. His own body, cool in the water, gave a single pulse from deep within. To distract himself, he pushed at the edges of the scarf he still wore about his waist, watching the cloth sink, then float back up to the water's surface.

Anteros rose, dripping and luscious, from his seat next to the floating Zeus. Water sluiced off his muscular body, poured from his tight buttocks. He flexed his wings, shaking them rapidly, and cool air fanned Zeus's hot face.

He tried to listen, making himself quiet inside, still. His senses were those of a god. When he focused, he could hear all, even the tiny footsteps of spiders in the glade where he grew up, the telepathic hum of ants, the burrowing of worms in the earth, the slow-growth stretch of trees.

He did not feel wrong to listen. If Eros and Anteros had not wanted him to hear them, they would have left.

Eros: "How is he?"

Anteros: "Relaxed. Calm."

"You did well, then."

"We must do better. He is sensitive. And in future, you will not want this one as an enemy."

"What care do I have of enemies?"

"None. But better to have lovers, yes?"

Zeus missed Eros's response, hearing only a garble of speech. Then he realized the two had switched languages. It took him a moment to pick up on the new tongue, but he had already missed some of what they were saying.

"...like all the rest in Tartarus," Eros was saying.

Zeus had heard the word Tartarus before. He was a primordial. But now his god-mind received some more meaning already seeded in his mind from birth, and he saw flashing images. A black gate tall as the sky. Labyrinths carved of the dark itself. Cobwebs thick enough to enfold a human being. Caves of foulness, skulls, and chains. Fires in oily pits. A sound like wind but not— it was the sound of living things suffering, crying, breaking. A disruptive swell of gravity as if the very place were pulsing, pumping, alive.

He thought Tartarus was a god. But what he was seeing was a place.

"He will not," Anteros said.

"My beloved, I will hold you to that."

What was that place of darkness? Aching? Horror? Like a dream he'd once had as a child. Adamanthea had told him it was nothing.

At the end of Zeus's vision stood two shadows shaped like cloaked humans, double his own height, hands upraised and holding balls of fire. Two sentinels. Two guards in a nightmare of a malignant abyss.

Zeus turned his head to look at Eros and Anteros. They, who had been talking of such darkness, such malevolence. They had been discussing him. Was he a part of that place?

For all that, they seemed unconcerned. Zeus held his breath as he watched Eros with his arm about Anteros's shoulders, pull him into his embrace. He leaned his head down and kissed him, long and open. His free hand moved down Anteros's body, caressing his bare waist, hip, thigh, and then back up again.

Zeus breathed. Slowly. In and out through his nostrils.

He could not look away as Anteros returned the embrace, turned his naked body, fully erect, into Eros, pressing himself against him. Fifteen paces away and still he could see the mist of arousal rise from Anteros's body, swirl the air, and thicken it.

Zeus's eyes grew heavy. That great pulse came again, deep from within him. His chest rose and fell. He turned back to face the water, the glimmer blinding to him, the little waves of it sloshing against his arms and ribs, cool, then hot, then wanting to ignite. He saw the flash before he felt it. The thunderbolt fled from his fingertips underwater, a sizzling green-gold flash, jagged and heart-stopping before it drowned in liquid depths, making the pool steam.

Suddenly, bare feet plunged into the water on the step. Anteros lowered himself into the pool, handing Zeus a golden chalice. "Here you go," he said, a tilt to his pretty lips. "Ah, the water's so wonderful and warm. Thank you, Zeus."

"I—I—" He'd lost control again.

Anteros shook his head. "Just drink." He grinned now, backing away on a wave of water, then plunging himself beneath its flickering surface.

Zeus put the sweet, red liquid to his mouth and drank.

*

He made sure to keep himself drunk, which made his lessons easier.

In only a few days, Zeus had lessons in knife-play, lasso, hand-to-hand, even wrestling, whereupon Eros took pity and allowed loincloths to be worn.

He learned astronomy, biology, chemistry, and the worst of the worst, technology that involved complex programs in horrible devices called computers, tablets, and communicators. And he learned something called "rocket science" which was ridiculous until it started to make sense. Still, the physics confounded him.

Though he still released, unchecked, random thunderbolts from his hands, especially when he felt the pulse of arousal, he grew stronger in his mental faculties, his ego. He learned to aim his internal heat and power towards water if he was in the fountain room, or towards the inner walls of the abode if there was no water to be found.

"The bolts are strong," Anteros told him, "but you'll have to get a lot stronger before you could do any real damage to this place. By then, you'll have more control. And Cronus will quake."

Zeus tried not to worry about Cronus, but he could never forget the constant threat of his father. He needed more power, more control, for eventual combat.

Anteros hinted that it would help if Zeus would simply allow him to assist him in the area of arousal release. That was where true power could be released, controlled, and released again, so he said. Zeus declined.

On that subject—arousal, ignition of power, blooming to become all he could be—all he could think of was Eros. For that, he wanted Eros and only Eros to be his teacher. But Eros, though he continued his lessons with Zeus in a gentle and polite manner, said nothing about Zeus's sexual awakenings.

He had dreams of gliding, flying, falling. Sometimes it seemed he swam for hours through unending dark. Repeatedly, he dreamed of that afternoon he'd seen Eros pulling Anteros to him, caressing his naked hip under the fluttering moth wings, and kept picturing Anteros's full, flowering erection on Eros himself. He woke with stickiness on his belly, yet no feeling of relief.

He thought, as he stared at Eros over the next days, this might be what falling in love felt like.

In the evenings before he slept, he lounged on soft couches and soaked in the magic candlelight of the floating mansion. He drank white and red and lavender ambrosia, all slightly different, each one better than the last, while the Erotes took turns telling him stories of the universe, of the gods, and of what Zeus's true powers might hold in store for the future of life on Earth and the Cosmos itself.

He learned each of the names of the Erotes, although he never got to know any of them as well as Anteros.

Though all the Erotes had a similar look and coloring, Himeros had shorter hair than the rest, and lavender wings outlined in black like a butterfly. He was never still, always restless, running off with one of his brothers in tow to the nearest bedroom. Zeus learned Himeros was the god of impetuous love.

Hedylogos had white-blond hair, perfectly straight, that was so long it swept between his white-feathered wings and caressed his bottom like a tail. He had sharper features, but always smiled. That smile made him look young, tender, innocent. He called Zeus sweetheart and pet and godling. Honestly, Zeus didn't mind, especially when he learned Hedy was the god of pillow talk.

Hymenaios, the most slender of the six, kept his hair braided along his back, a bisecting line between his black-spotted, white wings. He had broad shoulders, large muscles in his chest, and sang in a voice of echoes that billowed like a caress in the mind. It was a voice unlike any Zeus had ever heard. He was a veritable winged siren, and the god of love songs.

41

Hermaphroditus had the softest features of them all, with curved lines delineating muscle, instead of hard tendons or sinew, and his eyes curved downward as well, looking sometimes sad, sometimes shy. His lashes were thick, a dark bronze, almost brown, rimming his eyes. His wings were the smallest of all the Erotes, feathered and white but with no hard edges. The wing tops curled down at the tips. Herm was the god of male and female united. Anteros told Zeus Herm had two complete sets of male and female sex organs, but all that showed were the male organs, and the others still called him "he" whenever they referred to him. He didn't seem to care.

The last Erotes, Pothos, had the darkest hair, brown with stripes of copper, and eyes the color of storms, but were neither dark blue, nor black, but something in-between. His feathered wings were more silver than white, and smooth like a moth's. He had no other coloring on them. He meditated a lot, never bothered by any noise the others might make if they were all in the same room. He spoke the least, smiled the least, but enjoyed the antics of his brothers, embracing them often in the pool, or in the halls, his affections intense, serious, almost desperate. Pothos was the god of absent love. He breathed the air of longing.

They all called themselves the Erotes. But often, when Eros called for them in the early mornings and Zeus was awake and wandering the halls, the words he heard were, "Amoretti, my Amoretti, wake. Awake." Like a lullaby, the sound of his voice wove through the halls and rooms, making Zeus feel warm and comforted. One by one, the sleepy Erotes would come out, naked and tousled, ready for a breakfast of ambrosia, ready for a swim, and first-of-the-day antics.

When Zeus wasn't learning from Eros, Anteros rarely left his side, becoming a friend, a companion, and a voice for all the questions Zeus forgot to ask of Eros.

His next favorite to watch was Pothos. Zeus wasn't sure why, but he liked the god's more solemn nature, -- such a lovely god of longing—and the earnestness of his gaze. It seemed to

Zeus, who had a lot of time to observe, that Pothos's favorite brother was Hedy, the god who loved endearments. Often, they went off together, not to be seen for hours.

Ever more curious, Zeus followed them a couple of times, and stood outside their open room as they made love, listening, sometimes looking, sometimes longing to join them.

It happened again, one late afternoon, when most of the Erotes were dozing by the pool and Eros was away. Pothos and Hedy, lounging side by side, clutched hands, rose and wandered away. Zeus followed, far back down the cool hall, slowly approaching the bedroom where they so often slept together. His bare feet made no sound. His curiosity was quiet, innocent—so he told himself. Unobserved, in secret, Zeus had no qualms about watching them.

As he approached the open archway, he stopped just short of the entrance, hugging the wall with his back. He heard whispers and laughter, soft covers thrown to the floor, gasps and kisses. He heard Hedy say, "Thos, my love, my sweetest," and then silence.

Pothos said, low and almost grumbling, "I think you taste of peaches today."

After awhile of listening to the softest, silken sounds of caressing, the groans of pleasure, Zeus felt confident enough to edge his face along the threshold and peek inside the room.

Pothos lay on his back, silvery wings splayed on either side of him like a cushion against the bed. His long, lean body gleamed as he breathed and strained, fists clutching at his own feathers, legs spread. Hedy crouched between his thighs, head moving up and down. Zeus could see everything, the hard cock, shiny and wet as it left Hedy's mouth, his full, pink lips, his cheeks hollowed as he moved up and down on it. Sometimes Pothos thrust up, as if he could not control himself. Hedy would take him all the way into his mouth, despite the length of the cock, swallowing. Then Hedy would rise and suck on the tip, making Pothos moan and toss his head.

Hedy's hair tangled in his white wings, but was long enough to still spill over, glossy and shimmering, against his raised, perfectly curved buttocks as he suckled his lover.

They were utterly picturesque, the two of them like works of art—the art of fucking, and Zeus forgot for a few moments to breathe.

Pothos let out a strangled cry. Hedy's lips tightened upon him, pulled up with a sweet, erotic sound, and Zeus saw Pothos come, the white spray pulsing from the tip of his cock, five, six, seven times in succession as Hedy stroked everything out of him that he had to give. Hedy murmured words over and over, "My beauty. My love. My heart."

It might've all seemed ridiculous to Zeus if it wasn't so magical in the moment, a context in which nothing was strange, all was fluid and graceful and perfect.

Pothos flipped Hedy onto his back and returned the favor. Hedy's cock bobbed up, pink at the tip, dark copper at the base. Zeus could see the rounded balls were drawn up tight in arousal. His own cock pulsed at the sight.

Pothos engulfed him in his mouth and sucked eagerly. Hedy's wings were pulled tight to his sides, covering his arms. His hands were raised between his legs, holding Pothos's head, running his fingers through his fine, light brown hair.

Pothos pulled off Hedy's erection, letting it sway back toward his abdomen, put his hands under his lovely bottom and pulled him up. Zeus saw Pothos suckle the balls, slow and deliberate. Hedy murmured more endearments.

Zeus's skin grew hot.

Pothos moved up the cock with his tongue, finally taking it in again, sucking up and down until Hedy gasped. Pothos moved off, stroked him and licked at the tip. Hedy's cock twitched and spurted straight into Pothos mouth. Pothos drank every drop.

But they were not done. There was no stopping the two of them. Zeus knew they could go all afternoon. They were, after all, gods.

44

Pothos pushed Hedy up in the bed, folded his legs up against his chest and spread his buttocks. Pothos licked there for awhile, then pulled his own knees up and positioned his still hard cock against Hedy's crease. He pushed. Zeus could not see the entrance to Hedy's body from his vantage, but he did see that the cock went along the buttocks and disappeared. Then Pothos was up against Hedy's body, pulling him into his arms, kissing him. A slow fucking began. Zeus watched Pothos's hard cock go in and out of Hedy's body. Hedy's cock strained against his belly, bobbing up every now and again. He was loving it.

After a long time, while again Zeus forgot to breathe, Hedy stretched out his legs and said, "Turn me over. Take me from behind."

Pothos pulled out, cock glistening, the head swollen almost purple, the foreskin pushed all way down by the length and hardness of his erection, and Hedy turned over, presenting his perfect bottom, the rounded cheeks, and the plush but muscular thighs. Hedy angled himself a little more to one side, and suddenly Zeus could see the gaping, dark hole into his body. Pothos steered the head of his cock against it and pushed it in. Hedy rocked back, crooning. Pothos moaned.

Zeus let out a breath to see such a thing. It was quite lovely, and they could go for hours. Surely they would have welcomed him, had he entered the room and shyly asked for attention. But Zeus could only see Eros in his thoughts, in his dreams, and had no desire, or courage, to deviate from that fantasy.

Pothos fucked with a grace and strength that was mind-numbing. He thrust faster and Hedy bucked back to meet him every time. Joined cock to ass, they became one flowing person, reading each other's minds, knowing each other's feelings, pleasures, and hearts as true lovers should.

Zeus smiled. They would be at it for hours. Finally, he turned away to head back to the pool.

As he looked up to the end of the hall, he saw Eros in his green robe standing there, looking at him. Zeus's mouth fell open, but as swift as an eye blink, Eros was gone.

Amazing that he could do that, jump from location to location.

When Zeus got back to the pool, the other four Erotes were still dozing. Eros was nowhere to be seen.

Chapter Five

Eros raised his hand toward the wall, gave a slight wave, fingers curled halfway to a fist, and the black mark vanished.

Zeus stood beside him, head down. His fingers still burned from the accidental release of yet another thunderbolt. There had been no water. The bolt had hit the room's white wall. Roses had been blooming there and were now withered to black ash.

"Do not chastise yourself. You have made progress."

"I've made no progress! My control is as it was when I was twelve. If I get angry, or frustrated or—"

"Aroused?" Eros offered with a half-smile.

Zeus took a step away. Eros did not usually bring up the subject. The room they stood in was a library filled with carved wooden tables with lion claw feet, wall screens with live action art, rows of shelves with slick books. Some of them were the written word and some displayed moving pictures. The air smelled faintly burnt from all the machinery, but mixed in was a scent of sawdust, old leather, and ancient longings. Luckily, Zeus's mishap had not destroyed any of the room's precious items or technology.

"Zeus," Eros said softly. "You are here to receive lessons on all things. Including sexual desire. And you have learned so much. But in that area—" He paused. "You watch my six essences interact. They have offered to include you in anything, everything. Yet you decline."

"I know what they do. I understand their actions. That should be enough education."

"Perhaps."

Zeus looked up. "You are not insisting I participate, are you?"

"I insist on nothing. I offer you what you need in them. It is up to you to take it."

"But you yourself have never offered me a lesson in that subject, yet you are the god of love."

Zeus's cheeks heated at his bold statement. He hadn't meant to speak so bluntly, or accuse Eros of neglect. In this area Eros had shown no personal interest in Zeus, yet all Zeus did was dream of him. Want him. But to not be wanted back? It was the worst feeling.

Zeus's arms tingled. Energy grew again, deep inside. He tamped it down.

"I can tell you why," Eros said.

"I know why. You are a great god. A primordial god. I am nothing compared to that."

"Not true, or I would never have taken notice of you, let alone allow you into my home. Come sit with me." Eros approached one of the wooden tables.

Reluctantly, Zeus followed. They sat before a pile of books that smelled of oldness and dust, most of them comprised of sewn-together parchments. Their bindings were disintegrating. A small energy field held them together, making the edges fuzzy, soft-focused. There were amazing records, kept by hand and in computer form from ages distant or lost, even civilizations from other stars Zeus could not conceive of, containing history, poetry, battle maneuvers.

Zeus placed his forearms on the table, flexing his fingers, trying to discern the power in them. Right now, they felt normal again. He stared at them, the tanned backs, the pink fingernails, unable to meet the vibrant, emerald eyes of his teacher.

As Zeus tried to move his mind away from the present, and his inner turmoil, Eros began to speak. It was not what Zeus expected. The words were incredible.

"Do you not realize I think you are beautiful, talented, and desirable? Of course, I do. Zeus, you are lovely, enticing.

48

When I look at you I feel as I did when I was newly awakened in the Dark Abyss."

Zeus lifted his head. He did not—could not—believe those words. He waited for Eros to continue.

"But there is a fate in you."

His body slumped. This did not sound good. "I know what fate is. But what do you mean? What fate is in me?"

"At this moment, I would not like to say. I feel it is best that you are not influenced on this by what oracles and prophecies might think they know. Or even by my opinion, my feelings."

"That's not fair. If there is some impending destiny for me, shouldn't I know? Does it have to do with my father and the confrontation you say I must have?"

Eros sighed, which was a rare sound. Eros was so patient, never seemingly frustrated. "In part. And what the oracle said about your father is already beginning. But it's far, far beyond that, too."

"My far destiny is nothing unless I survive," Zeus hissed.

"You cannot die, but you can be contained. Held captive. And it may be a long time, years, millennia, before you approach your true destiny. No oracle can know for sure about all details or exact timings. But they do know trends and patterns and they are rarely wrong. I can tell you your fate is both a strength and a burden. Its potential predicts great benefit. I would not stand in the way of that."

"Stand in the way? But you are helping me."

"Yes."

"Then I don't understand what you're trying to say."

Eros leaned back, spreading his white wings on either side of the chair-back. He crossed his arms in front of his chest and contemplated Zeus with a narrow look. The muscles in his bronze arms flexed above his wrist where the sleeves fell away to the elbows. But though his brows had come together, his eyes were soft, like deep pools of warm green water, and Zeus felt pulled toward that gaze, that beauty. His skin prickled as if tiny

49

flames ran up and down his arms, legs, back. He was glad for his tight loincloth where nothing was allowed to move.

Finally, Eros responded. "I am saying, Zeus, that you are so beautiful and so young that I do not want to interfere with your growth."

Zeus shook his head. Shy but frustrated. Yearning but afraid. "I have a fate in me that you don't want to touch. That's what I'm hearing."

"Not exactly."

"I wouldn't want to tarnish you, of course." Zeus could not believe how petulant, how bitter he sounded. Immediately, he wanted to apologize.

"You have a burden of dark to light, Zeus, which is yours and yours alone. You must fight hard to keep it, fight the dark that overtakes you at times, but keep it for times you need great strength. If I were to become—ah, close to you, I would link to you. I would not see that restrain you in any way. I would not ever feel tarnished by you in any way, but I would not want you tarnished by me before you face Cronus."

Was Eros actually saying he cared for Zeus? And that his caring was too great, that it might be a hindrance to Zeus? It was insane, all of it. Zeus's desire. His kidnapping to this estate in the stars. His destiny to fight an insane god who was his father.

"I can't imagine you would tarnish me," Zeus whispered.

Eros started to stand. "You are dear to me. Never forget that."

Was this the end of the lesson then? Was Eros saying he would never love Zeus? Or rather, love him, yes, but never take him. Never be lovers. Zeus saw the six Erotes as emanations from Eros of different kinds of love, but the one missing was unrequited love. Perhaps there was another god for that, separate and alone. It would be fitting if Zeus met and fell in love with *him*.

Zeus started to rise as well, wanting to ask about that seventh god, but remained silent when Eros raised his hand.

"Stay awhile. Read this." He gestured toward a book of fine, thin paper sitting to Zeus's right. The book was in a language Zeus did not recognize, but in a moment his mind made sense of the scribbles, and he could read it, understand it. The title: *Wisdoms of Love*.

When Zeus looked up, Eros was gone. He had not heard him leave, not even the soft wisp of his robe shifting on bare skin, or on dry library air.

It did not take long to read the book. Zeus's mind absorbed knowledge the way a desert landscape inhaled water.

The book contained poems, stories, short sayings. Some of the stories were wildly erotic, depicting graphic scenes of sex. Others were about lovers who sacrificed something they loved for each other, or whose passion grew from ecstasy to stale boredom. One story told of a graphic rape and confinement.

Still more stories depicted betrayal, possession, and grief. Only a few had happy endings.

There were poems about great battles for beautiful women. About men who loved each other and died too young, also usually in battle. Broken hearts spilled all over the pages, little maxims spoke of love and courage, what love is like when all passion has fled, how love opens the heart to knowledge. Some poems concluded all love was a dirty trick. Others stated it was the most glorious of experiences, and to not experience it was a crime. The final statement on the last page was that love seeks to cultivate, not dominate.

Zeus left the library, thoughts warring. He wanted Eros. He wanted love. But what was he to take away from the lesson? That all love was doomed? That Zeus was not capable enough to survive anything that might happen as a result? Was this why Eros was rejecting him?

But why should love make him weak? He didn't understand.

He moved to the fountain room, needing a cool swim now, wanting to drown his confusion in the company of beautiful naked men and fresh bathing, even if it tempted him beyond endurance.

Love hurts. He scowled at the thought.

Anteros sat at the edge of the main pool, drinking ambrosia. Hedy and Thos were swimming circles about each other, slick and graceful as dolphins. The other three winged Erotes were missing.

Anteros greeted Zeus with a friendly nod. Zeus moved around him, saying nothing, and dived into deepest area of the scintillating water. A rushing embrace of coolness and relief surrounded him. There was a slight sting against his eyes as he opened them in his new silent world where everything floated, where he felt instantly serene.

Still, his mind would not let go of his conversation with Eros. He, Zeus, was the problem. Because he was not born ordinary, because he was a god with a destiny, and with power that grew its strength from darkness more than light, Eros held himself away.

It wasn't fair.

Night after night, Zeus had had dreams about Eros until he woke sweating and hard. In the first days, he'd managed to convince himself it was just an over-reaction to a new life, to the ambrosia, to a teacher whose knowledge seemed to span the cosmos.

But the obsession had grown, not receded as he'd hoped. He wanted Eros to reach out to him. To look at him. To touch him. All he could think of, day in and day out was Eros's touch. He could distract himself with lessons when Eros was around, but often his feelings grew too quickly, and the lightning arced.

It was the worst feeling.

It was the best feeling.

It was not to be allowed.

As he swam and thought about the day, about the book of love wisdoms, the water grew warm and fizzy about him. His body tingled.

Basically, Eros had intimated that nothing would or could happen between them. Eros himself would not allow it. Zeus's strength might be tainted by him.

Tainted? By Eros? Never.

These thoughts only frustrated him more. Anger brewed.

Before he succeeded in completely boiling the pool water with his emotions, he slid up over the edge and sat, dripping, his legs dangling only ankle-deep now.

"Zeus," Anteros said softly at his side, as if sensing his thoughts.

He saw out the corner of his eye Anteros's feet and firm, tanned calves as the winged man stood over him. Eros had called him Amoretti. Eros would never call Zeus such a precious name. Zeus's insides burned at the unfairness of it.

"I understand, Zeus," Anteros said softly. "We all do."

"What!" The word came out more like a curse than a question.

"We're all in love with him. It can't be helped."

"But," Zeus said, kicking hard at the water. "I'm not one of you and never will be. He said as much. Nothing will come of this, so I can do nothing about it."

Anteros bent his knees and hunched closer to Zeus's side. "We are like your brothers now. We love you. Why will you not allow us to alleviate your frustration?"

"I want to deal with this on my own."

"In isolation? In such an unhappy state?"

"What do I have to be happy about?"

Zeus turned his head to look at Anteros. How beautiful the lesser god was. How serene, with his moth wings and slender, youthful muscles, his half-erect penis so rosy and sweet, his coppery hair braided back on one side, his eyes the color of bright mica. Superimposing Eros over the nude god's visage, Zeus was suffused with an ecstasy of longing. And vexation.

"I am a god born to defeat his own father. I am to battle and possibly lose myself into darkness forever. I have a fate and a destiny. Eros said so himself. And I hate it!"

"I know, and we all want to help you. Even Eros."

"This isn't Eros's fight. Or yours. This is my life and I have to live in it."

"Come." Anteros held his hand out palm up. "Please." He stood.

Not quite trusting, still Zeus took the hand as Anteros pulled him up to stand. He led him to a buffet where pitchers of ambrosia stood, cool moisture beading on the crystal decanters.

Zeus was always thirsty. Anteros poured the pink mixture into a chalice and handed it to him.

"I know that one is your favorite."

It was some concession that Anteros had taken the time to learn that small detail about Zeus. He wondered if Eros knew it.

"I have to get him out of my mind," Zeus mumbled.

"We have all said the same at least once a year for uncounted years. And much more often when we were new."

"How old are you?"

"I cannot really say. Gods move in and out of time. Sometimes we go off to sleep for a hundred or more years. Standards for time change over eons. I could say I was a thousand years old and I'd be wrong. My memories span maybe five hundred of those years unless stimulated by a visual aid to go back further."

"Really?"

Anteros nodded. "Even then, I might not remember an event as more than a myth, a story. A god's brain is great, but even it is limited in the amount of memory and information it can hold. It can go on an irregular dump."

"That sounds terrible."

"It will happen to you, too."

They made their way to an alcove couch with plush pillows striped blue and white. The light on the water reflected

54

on the wall above the couch, making white-dappled ghost-lace that shifted as if pushed by some invisible wind.

They sat. Anteros pushed his naked thigh up tight against Zeus's thigh.

"It is not terrible. Not really. We are self-renewing. I wake every morning eager as a youth. How else could immortality be endured?"

"This will happen to me?" Zeus asked.

"Yes. It will."

"But I want to know everything. I want to remember everything."

Anteros's smile was like a light coming from within. "Some call that delusions of grandeur."

Zeus started to frown.

"But—" Anteros held up his hand in a friendly gesture. "Your grandeur is very real, Zeus. You are different. Special."

"How?"

"Power, for one. It is intense in you and a part of your great beauty. Most intelligences in the universe are still plagued by shallow-thinking, especially among the gods. Beauty gets the most reward. It is unfair, but a bitter truth. Do you not see how attracted I am to you at all times?"

Zeus brought the chalice to his lips to avoid answering. He did not believe it. Beautiful? Him?

But his eyes saw everything. He could not help but stare at the lovely body next to him, scintillating and ready, aroused and open. It made him quiver deep within. It made him hunger.

He wanted Eros.

But almost as much, he wanted to ice the fever, soothe the passion so he could be clear again, focused. But he was afraid. If he let it all out, would it not grow? Would it not become something out of control and even more distracting along with his errant power?

Anteros reached out and lightly touched Zeus's thigh. Zeus did nothing for a moment. Then he stood abruptly. "I need more to drink."

"Bring the pitcher," Anteros said.

Zeus had a short time during his trip to the buffet and back to the couch to decide to stay or go. But he really liked Anteros, and most especially his body liked Anteros. He could not deny it.

He poured himself more ambrosia, drank it down, refilled the pitcher with the pink version, and brought it back to the couch.

His head was swimming. He loved the feeling of his body going languid, being a little off-balance, and suddenly he laughed. He sat abruptly on the floor at Anteros's feet, placing the pitcher between them. Surprising himself, he leaned the side of his head against Anteros's knee. He knew he was drunk now. He didn't care.

His cheek rubbed against the bare flesh, skin to skin, smooth and alluring. Anteros in his arms would be like holding sunlight. Smooth and warm. Life-giving. Anteros would be summer sparkle against his skin.

He drank down his ambrosia while Anteros remained very still beside him.

If Zeus turned his head just right, he could see the jutting pink cock between Anteros's legs, firm and quite gorgeously formed. It was not too big, but not small. Zeus's own was bigger, but he was also taller, broader. Anteros was slender, sylph-like.

He saw tight golden curls at its base. A shiny, rose-colored tip protruded from the taut foreskin. Zeus had an impetuous thought to push all that skin down and see the rest. A voice inside him kept saying, *Touch him.*

In his mind, he saw Eros in the library saying, "You have a fate in you."

Zeus was already tainted, stained, marked, so how could Eros say his own touch might taint him more? But Eros would not touch him. It hurt. He wanted. He wanted so badly.

He drank ambrosia straight from the pitcher now, heard Anteros whisper, "Easy." But Anteros would never tell him he'd had enough.

The pool's pale shadow-light glimmered on the wall above Anteros's head. Shutting his eyes, the light behind Zeus's lids became blazing comets. Those comets burrowed into his veins and ran all up and down his body, leaving his skin feeling as if it were steaming.

Touch him.

He saw Eros in his mind, that magnetic green stare. But Eros would not have him.

Slowly, he turned his head until his chin pressed to Anteros's knee. With a soft push, he nudged and the knee moved so that now the other side of his face met the even softer skin of inner thigh. Zeus was inches from the center of Anteros. The cock waved a little, darkened. Zeus saw a pulsing vein. Another slight rise of the magnificent organ. It was almost touching the flat abdomen, but gravity brought it forward just enough. Enough to—what?

He glanced up. Anteros's yellow-green eyes flashed. "Just a touch?" the love god whispered. "Only if you want."

Zeus lowered his gaze again. He brought his right hand up between Anteros's legs, fingers up, and brushed gently at the rigid cock. Warm, yes, and skin so tight, the organ like its own being, containing essence and feeling and need. Hunger.

He was just drunk enough. He could do it now, what he'd wanted to do. He lightly clasped Anteros's cock, brought his thumb and forefinger up to the head and gently pulled down the skin.

The head was ripe, a dusky rose, almost lavender, firm like a perfect plumb. Zeus brought his face up to it, smelled the richness, the slightly salty musk, then opened his mouth and let his tongue dart out to taste.

He heard Anteros inhale, but the god remained still.

Anteros was tart and sweet, damp at the tip, like a fruit Zeus had never tasted but now wanted more of. God-fruit.

57

Zeus let his tongue lick all over the head, lapping at the lovely satin texture, licking up where flesh folded in to a dent, tongue-tip exploring the tiny hole there and the rounded smoothness on either side. A bit of fluid pulsed upon his tongue, like bitter salt. Like wine. His fingers moved lightly along the shaft. His tongue liked the taste and before he knew it his lips were on the skin about the hole, his tongue probing, his mouth automatically suckling.

He'd learned a lot from watching Hedy and Pothos.

He heard another gasp, louder this time. He was naïve, but he knew he was not hurting the god. Anteros's gasp communicated pure delight.

Zeus sucked a little harder and was rewarded. More elixir. Fine and pure. Anteros's hips jerked. The beautiful golden-pink cock with the lavender head slid deeper into Zeus's mouth as if it was a natural fit, and he didn't mind at all. He allowed the thrust and sucked it in further, feeling the life-pulse there, the hot throb of it.

Was Anteros going to come?

The thought of that, and the experience of the cock deep inside his mouth now, made his own already hard cock jump in its damp scarf-wrap. His whole body burned, but not from thunderbolts. Not right now. He wasn't afraid of that anymore. He focused and he sucked, and he gave Anteros pleasure. That was important. All of a sudden, he wondered why he had been so afraid. He'd been shy, of course, being the new god. The youngest god. But his reticence also had everything to do with Eros. He had wanted the primordial god's attention so badly that he'd mostly spurned the Erotes. They did not deserve that, but Zeus had been too mesmerized to see it. It was the only explanation he could think of.

He heard Anteros release a soft moan. It was beautiful. Zeus wanted to hear it again. He tightened his lips and moved his mouth up and down the shaft of the sensitive cock, letting his tongue linger on the head every time it was partially out of his mouth.

The moan came again, and a single word.

"Zeus."

He loved hearing his name spoken like that, like a plea, like a wind-blown cry. He grew dizzy giving this pleasure. Beneath his tightly tied scarf, his own cock pressed and pulsed for freedom.

Anteros bucked into his mouth, gently but insistent. Then he said, "It's our first time. I don't want to—" There was a pause, a little whimper. "Take your mouth away, I'm going to come."

That only made Zeus want to suck harder. Did the god think he didn't want to taste his ecstasy? Zeus was hungry for it. He wanted to drink and drink until there was no more. But he felt Anteros's hand on his forehead, pushing him back. The cock left his mouth with a wet, sweet sound and began to squirt a fountain of white liquid that landed on Zeus's chin and chest, and dribbled onto his fingers which still milked the shaft.

Pale rosy skin encased in a sun-browned fist. Zeus marveled at the differences in their coloring. Where Anteros was gold, he was more tarnished bronze. He liked the way they looked together.

Little cries escaped Anteros's mouth. Zeus kept milking, wanting it all. He lowered his mouth to the head, sucking at the leftovers, licking at the final pearled drops. After a moment, he let go. He glanced up again, a little shy.

Anteros was still catching his breath. "Indeed," he said quietly, "your grandeur is not exaggerated."

"You are like drinking the essence of dawn."

Zeus did not know how he came up with those words. He had a sudden urge to run. But the room was filled with light, his mind a mist. His body seemed to hover above the floor. He felt himself falling back and suddenly there were more winged men all around him as if to catch him, all looking down at him, their glistening naked bodies merging and melding into a tapestry of interwoven golds. The most amazing thing Zeus had ever seen.

A voice said softly in his ear, "Lie back. Lie back."
Anteros.

A hand at his brow, warm and dry. Mingled scents of lavender, sandalwood, peach. And a little of the sea. More hands on his chest, belly, thighs, gently moving, massaging. Lips at his cheek.

He opened his eyes and saw Anteros kneeling beside him, wings up and fluttering, his scarf of hair brushing Zeus's face. Anteros moved his lips to Zeus's and kissed him sweetly, with gentle pressure.

Zeus felt the soft-spun cloth at his hips, which he'd made sure to tie very tight, loosen and fall away, and his hidden skin was exposed to the air, tingling, heating. The caresses on his thighs and belly sent a bolt of pleasure to his groin. His cock thrummed with his own pulse, hard, falling against his belly under its own weight.

Suddenly the Erotes were all over him. Their hands, their mouths. Fingertips caressed his balls. Lips sucked his nipples. Hands ran up and down his inner thighs. Something soft and wet touched the base of his cock and traveled up. Anteros kissed him on the mouth again. Again.

The air had wind in it and he knew it was made by the fluttering of all those wings, some feathered, some silken, all large and excited.

Zeus had a sensation of falling. When a hot mouth sucked down on his cock, he lost himself in pure whiteness, blind and thrashing. Whose mouth was it? Hedy's? Thos's? Or maybe Himeros, god of impulse. For this was impulse, nothing more. Drunkenness. Unruly behavior gone wild.

He wanted. He wanted so much, but not necessarily this, though it was good. But there was something missing. Something more that he wanted. Always more. For he was Zeus, and whatever that meant, he was different.

But could he afford to let go? Could he do this and wake and regain any sense of self? For he felt he was breaking up, coming apart.

60

Then the rapture hit. Euphoria. His cock jerked and pulsed in the most incredible way, and liquid burst from it. Not lightning. His seed. His essence. It kept pulsing, the impact grinding him into the floor in such overwhelming pleasure he thought it would never end.

Someone lifted his legs. High. He felt more caresses on his buttocks, and in between. Licks and lips. Tiny bites on his inner thighs. Fingers massaging. Mouths pressed his nipples, and Anteros at Zeus's own mouth, holding his face in his hands, gently kissing. His cock, though spent, still felt rigid.

It began again. The gentle licks up his shaft. The tease. Letting him feel it all slowly moving through him, that burn in his veins, that tingle in his belly, that jolt in his groin. He bucked up. A wet, hot mouth encased him again. Hands held his legs up. The mouth stayed with him. Another licked at his balls, then lower. Kisses pattered up and down his stomach, then to his thighs. He could not escape it. He didn't want to.

He had an unbidden thought. Was Eros watching? He hoped not. Then he hoped he was. But of course Eros knew everything that went on in his own home, with his own *amoretti*. He had already been told Eros could see through the eyes of his manifestations. Essences or tulpas or whatever sort of gods they were.

That meant Eros was surrounding him, on him, in him. And yet, the primordial god was not even in the room. He had all the benefits without the responsibility. He did not have to "taint" or be "tainted" by Zeus, from Zeus.

Suddenly he had the urge to run. From everything and everyone. It was as if he could not breathe. His mind grew dizzy. Anteros pressed his lips with more kisses and it was sweet but Zeus turned his head, blind, trying to think through the fog of sensation, and too much ambrosia.

"Stop," he whispered.

Anteros pulled back, but the hands still caressed, the tongues still licked. Fingers combed through his long, dark hair. "Relax."

"Stop. Please!" he said louder. Something began to burn higher up in his chest, an energy, a pounding force that made him grit his teeth, hold his breath. His throat tightened. Heat formed behind his eyes.

"Stop!" he cried out again.

Anteros lifted his head back and said, "Wait!" He was looking at his brothers. Giving an order.

The touches stopped.

But Zeus's panic did not abate. He pulled his legs up and against himself. Rolled to his side. It didn't help. He cried out at the pressure, at the great hollow feeling rising up within him. The thing that Eros would not or could not tell him about. The fate inside him.

He was shaking as he clasped his hands together, turned his head into the floor. Then the fire at his fingertips began to tingle, like bee stings all over at first, growing to a hot burn. It hurt. It hurt a lot. He rolled partially onto his back and raised his hands away from his chest. The lightning that burst from him was jagged, edged in green-orange flame. It flew from his hands, two thunderbolts, then three, then five, six, seven.

The ceiling crumbled where they hit. Dust, pebbles and large chunks of something softer than stone rained down on him. He could no longer feel or see the Erotes. He hoped they were running away. He blinked through heavy dust, trying to see where they might have gone when a large white chunk of the ceiling fell on top of him.

Everything went black.

Chapter Six

Someone's arms clasped him tight. His face was pressed to soft silk, and a firm chest. He lay limp, aching, thoughts murky. A slow rocking motion made him realize he was being carried. Like a baby. His big form was being cradled and held as if he weighed nothing at all.

Scent of rain and flowers. Autumnal thorn and leaves long left in a puddle. Sound of wings, a sort of cloth on cloth shushing, a tremble upon the air. A psychic sensation of vastness hit him, as if a friendly abyss of light had scooped him up. But there were wrinkles of shadow at the edges. Heat and light, yes. But a winter, too, within.

Nothing made sense. He had to be dreaming. But a cough welled up in his lungs and he knew this was real. Zeus shivered. Made a soft, strangled sound.

Eros's soft voice. "You are all right. The damage is great. But it will take me only a few minutes to fix it."

Zeus had no idea if Eros referred to damage to his home, or damage to Zeus himself. Maybe both.

He should have felt awkward in Eros's arms, but he was cradled just right, with no hesitation, and he had automatically thrown an arm under Eros's arm. His free arm rested over his chest.

The room that had become his room surrounded them, and he saw his own bed with the rumpled covers from the morning, the purple spread, and the white sheets. He saw the windows with their parted curtains showing a constant, starry night. The constellations of the far reaches invaded his mind. Couldn't he just go out there, faraway from all this, and be something else, live another life?

Eros placed him gently on the bed. Zeus did not miss the care he took, the concern in the green eyes, which came into focus as Zeus blinked. He thought Eros might simply go, but he sat on the edge of the bed, hands still on Zeus's shoulders, and raised them to his face.

"Let me." Soft. Comforting.

That was when Zeus realized his face hurt. It was wet, too, and when he tried to move his lips to utter any sound, he could not feel them. Eros's hands ran over his head, cheeks, jaw, and lastly his mouth, fingertips sliding over his lips until feeling returned, and the pain receded. Zeus then remembered the collapse of the ceiling upon him. He must have been hurt. Badly.

When Eros took his hands away, they were red. He reached somewhere alongside the bed and Zeus heard a drawer open. Eros drew a towel up and began to clean his hands. He looked back at Zeus and used the towel to gently wipe his face.

"You are fine now. You will need a bath later, though."

Zeus said, "I damaged your home."

"My Erotes are fixing it as we speak."

His vision blurred. Sweat began to drip along his temples, tickling the skin there, dampening his hair. He turned his head away, realizing he was lying naked in the bed, with Eros hovered over him.

A pain came over him, a rushing ache in his gut, a feeling of being covered in bee stings. He did not like this vulnerable feeling. He wanted to get up, to leave. None of this was working out. He was failing. Failing miserably. He would meet his father and lose, he was sure of it now, and he would be locked away forever in some supernatural stomach-prison, and that would be that.

"You need to rest a bit, and then things will be better."

"I cannot function. I cannot function." Zeus kept repeating the phrase, head turned away.

He curved his body away from Eros and drew his hands together, catching them between his legs. Eros came up over him, his strong arms enfolding him before Zeus could even react. And there he was again pressed to Eros's chest.

"Shh. I am here. I am sorry."

"Go away."

"Zeus—"

"I don't want you." He was embarrassed, naked, and still half-hard. Eros was looking at him. *Looking at him.* "And you don't want me!"

"Did I never tell you I love you?"

"What?" Zeus's face was pressed to the satin robe. Eros smelled of orchids blooming in sweet rain. Of absolute bliss. But why was Eros saying this now? Of course. It was just because Zeus was upset.

"I can feel you wanting to run. To leave forever. Please don't. We are only just getting started. You have done nothing wrong, nothing irreparable."

"I will never learn," Zeus mumbled. "I can't, not when you do this to me, like you are right now."

"I know you love me. I am your perfect teacher. You honestly believe that you can learn better from a teacher you do not love?"

"Yes. Because I am always confused! I am always so feverish!" He let his frustration pinch his voice.

Eros nodded. "I know, Zeus. I know all of that. It's how you grow up. It's what you have to go through. But you haven't had a chance until now. Harnessed all your life. That is not your fault, but it is not a way any being, god or man, should ever be treated."

Zeus gave an exasperated groan. Maybe he should be harnessed again. Maybe that was what he responded to. He'd been trying to harness his sexual energy by tying his loincloth too tight, as if his instincts told him that would be for the best.

He did not want to lie there like a baby and continue to whine. He wanted to be alone. But Eros would not allow it.

He tried to push Eros away. Eros was like a marble statue, heavier, actually. He did not budge at Zeus's god-strength.

"Your first sexual experience brought the house down, at least."

Zeus looked up. Eros was smiling.

"That's not funny."

"It is."

"But it—it—"

"What? Not good enough for you?" Eros teased.

"It should have been you."

A flash of glitter in the green eyes.

"I thought I explained that. The links I form with others through sex are not to be taken lightly. I do not wish to distract you from your future. You must have a clear mind and clear thoughts if you are to defeat Cronus."

"My mind is not clear. I am a complete failure right now."

"You are quite a mess, aren't you?" Eros looked at him as if he gazed upon something he had never seen before, and brushed the hair at Zeus's forehead. Just that gesture sent Zeus's body aflame. He began to shake.

"All right," Eros said. "All right. Relax. Look into my eyes and just be in the moment now."

Zeus's watery vision made the face of Eros softer. The gold hair looked as if it were decorated with tiny lights no bigger than grains of sand. Stars, maybe, yes that was it. Stars in his hair. His wings were drawn back and tight, white as foam, pristine and so perfect. Graceful. Stunning in their fine beauty.

"If I draw you to me now, all could be lost."

Or all could be won, Zeus thought. "I still don't understand—"

Eros put tapered fingers to his lips. "Listen to me, my sweet boy. What you face is so difficult for one so young, but you are a god. A strong god. The strongest I have ever seen aside from the primordials. What you need to do requires focus, no attachments, and no distractions."

Too late. "I am already distracted."

The fingertips pressed harder on his lips. "Shh. There are so many things you do not know."

Zeus pushed back against those fingers, raised his head.

"I understand that," he muttered. "If you're so strong, why don't you help me defeat him? On a physical plane where we can do something about it. The lessons are good but I'm done. I can't learn to control myself so I might as well face him with my rage. Unleashed, it took your ceiling. Is a Titan any worse?"

Eros took a breath, started to speak, and stopped.

Finally, he said, "Cronus holds much power. He rules all the Titans. He is not just one man. He is an army of men. Of course I will be helping you in ways you can't understand right now."

"Tell me!"

"No. Just listen. The real battle is between you and your father. He once ruled a realm of peace, both the Earth realm and the Cosmos. But he has done monstrous things. His mind is fragmented and he will not heal it, he will not go to his millennial rest. To the Lethe. He refuses, and no god can be forced to go there."

"That still doesn't answer my question." Zeus was feeling less shaky as he listened to Eros's voice. The room in low light grew into a haven. Zeus's anger and arousal subsided for that moment. The covers beneath him were soft. Eros's hand on his brow was light, a strange source of calm. He felt his question was almost rude, but he had to blurt it out. "Will you or will you not fight at my side?"

"I cannot. This is not how this plays out. You must face him alone or he will win. That is the prophecy."

"Why is that prophecy even considered? You are the strongest. There is nothing you can't do."

"The prophecy is true. You simply must trust me on this. Your battle is destined to take place in Tartarus. I cannot go there with you. If I do, Cronus will win. Cronus will take my strength and drain me. For this battle, you are the one with the strength, not me. You are the stronger one."

"You are not weak," Zeus replied softly.

"No. But I am the god of love. The strength of love is great. The torture of it is agony. Tartarus magnifies that agony a thousand times over and over. It will drain me to the point I will be of no use to you. Zeus, I am a good teacher for you, but I cannot be a good teacher if I know I am your distraction, and if I connect with you now, through love, through the link of sex, I will be with you in Tartarus in spirit, and that will weaken you. Tartarus will take that from inside you and warp it, make into agony. That is what that place is, but it is where you must have your battle. I know you do not understand. But please take my word in this. We cannot have a bond. You are dear to me. That is why I avoid you."

Things became clearer with such few words.

"You could have told me all this sooner." Zeus lay still, naked and vulnerable to Eros.

"You were not ready. You did not have the capacity to understand even a few days ago. You have to go through the feelings in order to fully dominate them. You have to be whole before you can be who you are, your truest self, who you are meant to be."

Eros seemed to be jumping ahead again. Zeus tried to follow. Who was he meant to be? What could it mean to be whole? Could anyone ever truly know themselves that fully after a lifetime, two lifetimes, or a thousand years?

It was true. He would not have been able to listen, to understand before. It took bringing the house down, and the eroticism of the winged and sun-struck Erotes, to finally awaken him. But even now he was undisciplined, and could see he needed more control. Even now he had too many misgivings, too much fear.

Zeus kept his voice low, and his body was strangely calm. "I am not ready now. Or maybe I never will be. I cannot control myself. I don't know what I'm doing. Cronus has every advantage."

"You cannot see what I and my Erotes can see. We do more than look at you. We look into you."

"But what do you see? What—who am I?"

"The power of the suns. The essence of void swept up into a swirl of netted stars so brilliant the eye cannot perceive it alone. I see a silhouette of stars and void, light and dark both cut out of reality when I look at you Zeus. I see a god who can walk on the very shards of light itself. I see the Cosmos. I see a ruler."

Zeus stared up at him, the winged god ignited in a luster only nature could manifest. A man of flaxen attributes brighter than the jewelry of all the stars. If Eros saw this in Zeus in return, maybe some day there would be hope for them. But now?

"I am all that?" Zeus asked. Eros's words were amazing, but disbelief ravaged him.

Eros nodded.

"But I am only eighteen. I am barely past boyhood."

"I know."

"But—"

"You have a dreamer's soul. You have purity of conviction. Something most gods, especially young ones, seem to be missing. For now it will have to be enough."

He still could not believe. He had no convictions that he could feel were real, only the fate Eros had earlier spoken of.

"But the fire in me—"

"Your power," Eros interrupted. "I've told you. It is a darkness, too. But handled well, you will thrive."

"I'm marred. Stained."

"Not yet. Everyone has these elements within. No one is exempt, not gods, not mortals. But some have more than others. Some have to work harder than others to handle it. Some give in to these mercurial elements altogether, living in utter chaos. But I see more than that in you."

I won't give in, Zeus thought, but even as young as he was, he knew the thought for the naiveté it contained.

Still feeling all too exposed and vulnerable, Zeus made a grab for a coverlet, but Eros stopped him with a soft touch to his wrist. His wings shifted, making a shushing sound upon the still air of the bedroom.

The room's light was tinged orange and it gave Eros's blond hair a darker tinge. His fingers, where they touched Zeus, were long and graceful. His arms were firm, going up into his sleeves, lovely muscles, smooth like marble woven through with trails of green-blue veins. All the Erotes were beautiful in their muscled, golden ways, but Eros had a skin color that looked lit from within. Zeus saw his own darker brown skin in contrast, where the fingers of Eros brushed, and wondered at their differences.

So many times in just the past few days it had seemed as if Eros read his mind. Now it happened again. "You seek to cover yourself, yet your beauty defies words. Are you shy about being admired?"

"I'm not like you, or Anteros or the others."

"What do you mean?

"I feel rougher. Darker. Unkempt. I belong to nothing, no one."

"You were raised bound and tied. You never had a chance to see yourself, to look, to be fascinated and perhaps content. It is not conceit to know the traits you possess are physically beautiful. Come stand with me, by my side, right now."

Eros gave Zeus a tug on the wrist and Zeus sat up, still with an urge to cover himself, at least from the waist down.

Zeus moved his legs over the side of the bed, feeling the soft coverlet press the backs of his thighs. He looked down and saw that his cock, nestled in shiny black curls, was mostly soft again, and was glad that at least he didn't have to be

70

embarrassed about that. But he glanced away from it quickly, and away from his powerful brown thighs that bunched as he stood.

Eros took his hand in his, even as Zeus tried to pull away. The feathers of those wings extended, brushing against Zeus's back, making the skin tingle. He felt it in his cock, which twitched, and blushed, his cheeks heating. He wanted so many things, to run from Eros's grasp, to hide, to rush headlong into life, to escape life, to be anyone but himself, to take hold of his power and all his rage and just let it explode over and over into the universe forever. So many feelings so fast. He felt helpless to master them all.

He realized he was shaking as Eros led him to a window, space-black, the spatter of stars across the abyss of infinity causing a lurch in his heart. In the hard, clear pane that separated them from the stars, Zeus saw a silhouette of his own dark reflection, and Eros beside him, white-winged and glowing.

Eros made a sweeping gesture with his free hand and the pane of stars turned into a solid silver window where Zeus looked face to face upon himself and Eros staring right back. Dark and light, side by side, they stood, Eros still clasping Zeus's wrist.

"Mirrors can teach. Mirrors do not lie. You have never had the chance to really look upon yourself. Today's lesson: I command you look. Here. At every aspect of yourself. Get to know it. See your beauty but do not fall into it."

Zeus frowned. Fall into his own beauty? He didn't think so. He could barely focus. Besides, he didn't think he was beautiful. Not compared to Eros and his Erotes. He was so different from Eros, un-winged for one thing, and still feeling awkward, stupid, uncontrolled. He did not want to look at himself. Couldn't bear it.

"I don't want this." He turned his head aside.

The grip on his hand tightened. "Do not look away from yourself. That is the first way to becoming irrevocably lost."

Eros let go of him, and moved slightly behind Zeus, hands on his head to turn him back to face the mirror, then the hands move to his shoulders.

"Look. Just look. No judgment. No expectation. The boy you are has become a man. A god. You need to look. To know. To understand how you are, what you are, and all the ways you respond and react to become the whole total of yourself. It will take a long, long time. You are many things, many aspects of a self. But first: the body."

Eros ran his hands down Zeus's arms from his shoulders to his elbows. At every touch, the flame in Zeus licked, heated, and grew. Zeus thought himself unremarkable, until Eros touched him. Then he saw how the fingertips of the god seemed, as if by magic, to sculpt him. As if he had not come into being until the teacher shaped him. He saw how the muscles of his upper arms curved beneath the dark bronze of his skin, how that skin began to take on a sheen of dimension, not just a flat sun-brown tone.

Slowly, Eros's hands came back up and wove through the black hair that draped Zeus's shoulders, pulling it back, letting the fringe of it brush his forearms. His hair against Eros's arms took on a gloss he'd never noticed; the wave of his hair parted at his forehead a little to the left curving against his face and reflecting diamond and blue shades from the room's dim light like a black liquid.

Eros pushed his palms up to Zeus's face, framing it, and suddenly Zeus saw his eyes come alive, lit as if from within with a sparkle, as if the stars themselves lay behind the blackness of iris and pupils. He saw his own cheeks, full with youth, but not babyish, lighten, lift, and the jaw firm and hard, two lines angled toward an almost square chin.

"Look."

Eros's hands smoothed over Zeus's chest and he saw the delineation of muscles and deep lines beneath his pecks, ribs, and his flat stomach quivering as he tried to keep his breathing steady, slow. His skin seemed to waver in its heat, its sensitivity to touch, its alive-ness apparent. His cock began to fill.

He thought about being embarrassed but he was more focused now, and Eros had already seen him at all levels of emotional upset: drama, tears, fury, drunkenness, and arousal. He could not hide from him. Never had been able to.

"Look." Eros's voice whispered over him, softer now, everything effortless, the stresses momentarily gone, the fire in Zeus quenched for the moment into mere lightning-bug sparks, only the tiniest of burns now deep inside his chest.

He looked upon the firm legs the held him up, his form growing greater in the mirror, bigger than Eros who was tall but more lithe; whereas Zeus was darker, more muscular, with a young man's new passion in his dark brown eyes. Nothing to be embarrassed about and everything to admire.

"You are one of the lucky," Eros's voice rustled against his skin like a thin, sweet breeze. "I do not make such statements lightly, Zeus. I do not have to, for I am a primordial god and I do as I wish. I do not waste my time with foolish children or jealous shallow gods. I do not choose who I admire lightly. But don't let all of this go to your foolish head, either. You may be a teenager yet and still, your experiences limited to an unnatural childhood, but you are smart and you need not act like so many of the gods do, manipulative, interfering, childish in their temperaments and their spoiled desires. You can choose to be better. Look at yourself and decide. Who will you be?"

Now Zeus did look. Deep and long. At himself. At his body. At his dark visage in the mirror. He was as Eros said. Magnificent. He could not deny the fact, though a part of him still wanted to be like Eros and his Erotes, brother to them, blond and golden, winged and seductive, he saw in himself other attributes to satisfy himself. He was not completely unfortunate-looking, or hopeless. In fact, just the opposite.

Though stream-lined, narrow-waisted, narrow-hipped, he had bulging curves of muscles on his arms, chest and thighs. He looked strong, like a true warrior. And his face, he decided,

73

with the right tilt of his mouth and a firm set of the jaw, could beguile. Beauty, to him, was Eros, through and through. But in himself he saw a dark echo of Eros, the beginnings of a realization that beauty, as a general definition, did in fact define his form as well as strength.

Finally, Zeus met Eros's gaze in the mirror, straight-on, unblinking.

For a moment they connected in that way, each to each, power to power, and Zeus felt a different sort of throb from within, one that led to streaming futures he could feel but not see. One that seemed, with a hand of passion beyond the lust he'd just recently felt, to reach out and encase his heart.

His sudden shyness retreated. Air and light and power seemed to fill him up. He wanted to be whole like the incredible body he saw before him. He wanted to feel it deeply within. Defeating Cronus was only part of his new desire, the opening of his need to fight, to live not like a single bloom, but a whole field of flowers, their petals contracting.

The other part of his desire was for Eros to admire him, to see that he was everything and more, that Eros might imagine. He would do this battle for himself, and for Eros. For love.

He opened his mouth. The words came in a language combined of reverence, awe, conviction, and love.

"If I am as you say, then teach me everything you know."

Eros's lips pressed tight. His head shifted in an almost imperceptible nod.

Chapter Seven

Zeus spent every new day training, reading, or soaking in the pool. He drank ambrosia almost faster than the Erotes could bring it to him. He seemed to inhale knowledge, experience and skill. He was calmer now, and had fewer accidents with his lightning bursts.

He still dreamt of Eros every night. But his experience bringing the roof down, and his private talk with Eros, had woken something in his too-shocked mind. He was now able to quiet his thoughts a little easier. He was still afraid of his father, but the fear gave him a determination instead of just confusion and panic.

He discovered new things about himself. He was good at most everything he attempted, but learned that his favorite lessons included archery, swimming; and reading subjects such as the histories of many cultures, including other worlds; battle strategy on land, sea and in space; poetry; music; philosophy. And he still enjoyed watching Hedy and Pothos make love.

Now his days were filled with many new things. He was able to focus more. And his physical body continued to fill out to a true and mighty god's proportions.

He knew he should feel proud. But a deeper part of him still felt aimless, lost. He did not know how to express this continued unease to Eros, who intimated all of Zeus's problems began and ended with Cronus. Perhaps he was right. For if Zeus could defeat the threat of his father, he would be free to move on in his own right as a god of the Cosmos with all the rights and power that entailed. He would be able to choose a real life, any he might want. And he might be able to continue to capture Eros's attentions.

On that last topic, he felt the biggest burden. He had never wanted anything more in his life than the white-winged god at his side. Every day that he trained with Eros was a pleasure. And it seemed to him that Eros felt the same.

The frustration of wanting more, though, spurred him on, continued to push and pull at his mind and heart. Every day he felt stronger, able to move through his deeper feelings and not allow them to distract from the more urgent task at hand: the Titan god who wanted to ensnare him in his massive form, into his stomach, and thus hold Zeus captive with his brothers and sisters for all of time without end.

He sparred with Eros in the sawdust of the arena where he'd learned wrestling, archery, and the staff. They used real swords, heavy and jeweled, and the gemstones in the handles flashed as they moved with a speed and agility only gods could manage. Even though neither could really die, they had blunted the tips. After all, a god could still feel pain.

Zeus was still weaker than Eros in skill, but he learned quickly.

Eros and Zeus circled each other. Eros's wings were held tight to his back. It looked almost as if he had nothing but down-covered flesh from shoulders to thighs. He wore only a strange, tight loincloth that hugged his lean muscles from upper thighs to the dents of his hip bones. His skin gleamed with thin moisture, breathtaking.

Unlike Eros, whose body had yet to hit the floor, Zeus, swaddled in his familiar silver scarf, was covered in sawdust as he whirled and danced through his mistakes, always learning.

He landed hard on his back, quickly regained his breath, and turned and spun through the air before Eros could tap him on the chest as he had so many times before. This was a first for the day. He'd escaped. Eros was quick, so Zeus considered escaping the tap a victory.

He glanced up for a second at the benches on a raised dais at one end of the room. All six Erotes had come to watch the sparring session. Their beautiful bodies leaned forward, elbows on knees, wings furled tight, their concentration and interest almost fierce.

While they were all gods of love, they certainly took interest in combat for defensive purposes. Anteros had told Zeus after one such intense session, "We love to watch Eros in sports because it's fun."

The beauty of Eros could not be disputed. But Zeus focused away from that entirely while training now. A distraction such as beauty would only mean failure for him and for his mission.

He could never hope to kill Cronus; the sword would be useless against him. But he did need to learn all he could in strategy, be it any sport or art. He needed to know how to move, how to distract, how to maim a god well enough to gain the upper hand. Cronus, he was told, would not hold back on any front, be it physical, mental, or magical.

Zeus had no idea how he, an eighteen year old god, could ever be any match for an old and powerful giant, and still had serious qualms.

After his session with Eros, he wandered the arboretum, losing himself in the sound of the brook, in the green and yellow leaves of the mini-wood that Eros had constructed. He heard a rustle behind him, like trees in wind, and saw Anteros standing in a dappled glade, his moth wings fanning gold and tan upon the air.

Anteros offered a small smile. Zeus did not return it.

"Couldn't I just stay here forever?" he asked.

"Even here, you are not safe. Cronus could find you at any moment."

"Then I could remain on the run. Take one of those ancient starships from Alioth that I read about and glide through the stars for eons." Of course, then he'd be without Eros. A disappointment and alone.

Anteros said, simply, "Do you not think Cronus has access to such ships as well? He would follow. You would be caught. Eventually."

Zeus put his hands together, gripping hard. He tried not to sound ungrateful, but his situation seemed hopeless.

"I have been taught strategy and ideas, yet I have no strategy, no ideas. Eros has given me nothing but some books and lessons, taught me how the books of light work. And then told me the prophecy said I would succeed if I faced my father alone. That is it!"

"You are more prepared than you might think."

"I have no indication of that."

"You have one thing no one else does. You are Cronus's son."

"That is what makes me his enemy!"

"You are the one who escaped. The one who is grown now, the one he must face who can speak for himself, who can reason and fight, maybe even… love?"

"Love? You mean love my father whom I've never met and who wants to kill me?"

"Well, don't discount it yet. I am the god of love returned. Maybe I can help you."

Zeus let out an exasperated breath. "How?"

"First, we need to learn about him."

"Have you ever met him? Does Eros know him?"

"No. None of us Erotes have met him. Eros has, though. I know that Cronus's reputation as a ruler was once a good one once."

"What happened?"

"There is history on the Golden Age of his rule on Earth. We just have to find it in the library. Then you can learn about it."

"Why was I not reading this history from the moment you brought me here?"

"You have been here not two weeks, Zeus. Even a god can be overwhelmed. And first you needed foundations for every subject."

"What I need is every piece of information on Cronus that can be found. It's what I have always needed. Can Eros hear me through your ears, see me through your eyes? If so, tell him he has neglected this part of my education and ask him why!"

"He does not always see through us. Only sometimes." Anteros's features remained calm, even as Zeus felt himself begin to quiver, and the heat rose up inside him once more. He wanted to shake Anteros. He wanted to yell, to hit, to rage.

Why was he only learning now that he needed to actually get to know his father?

A flash of white seemed to burn into his eyes and all of a sudden Eros was in the glade with them, golden body framed by snowy wings. He wore only a white drape of silk across his waist.

"You are ready for strategy?" Eros asked, coming to stand in front of Anteros.

Zeus wanted to scowl, but the beauty of Eros held his mind rapt. He could not look away from the hardened muscles under the glowing skin, the piercing green-gold eyes, the pink lips. His stomach tightened. He could not purge his mind of the day Eros had held him, comforted him after he'd damaged the house. The memory of the feel of his skin, warm and smooth, roused him. He finally mumbled, "I was always ready."

"No. You were not. You would not have understood. Some things are only ready to be learned when the student begins to ask the right questions. You are quick. I thought it would take you at least another few days."

*

In the library, Eros gave Zeus more parchment tomes, as well as lists on books of light where all he had to do was touch a subject word and information flowed over the window pane.

"All this for something called *The Golden Age*?" Zeus asked.

"You are unlucky enough to have been born just a moment too late to experience it. An ecstatic time of everything in balance, perfection enhanced for all beings, mortal and god alike. No wants or pain or age. When mortals died, they simply went to sleep still in their beautiful, youthful guises and yet they lived long lives of pleasure and joy."

"What about greed? Envy?"

"Everyone knew the right things to do. Acceptance, generosity and love were law. Even for the gods who made love all day and drank joyously all night."

"Gods do that now," Zeus grumbled.

"Yes. And worse things, too. But in the Golden Age there was no war. No violence. No hatred. Philosophers have said there was also stagnation, less creation, less intelligence for it was not required. But who cares of one is happy all the time, living in bliss? Philosophers say the Cosmos exists to expand, to evolve. It cannot do that if will is pushed back by complacency. And yet, what is the reason for evolution? To keep trying to perfect creation, no? I was one of the critics endlessly philosophizing. Yet I also long to return to such a time. No words can describe the era, the golden days, the starry nights, and the people so loving it brings tears to my eyes. It was as if all the Cosmos was under a spell. Or drugged. It lasted 5000 Earth years."

"And Cronus ruled the Earth during that time?"

Eros nodded.

At 18, Zeus could barely conceive of the number 5,000 in years. Yet he would exist far longer than that. For now, he could not imagine it.

"I don't understand how such a horrible, destructive god could rule such a peaceful time."

"Loss, misery and worse can change us. The darkest of dark thoughts can make a mind malfunction. For mortals and for gods. But since we gods are immortal, our madness cannot outlast our eternal essence. These personal aberrations come and go. To cope, some gods sleep what we call the long sleep for hundreds, even thousands of years to awake refreshed again. Others take the drink from the river Lethe and start new lives, some even pretending to be human for a time. Lethe is, like the long sleep, a short-term answer. The effects cannot last forever in a god. We are fated—or some say fortunate—that we will be the ones to experience everything eventually, in a linear fashion."

"Is that true for all? For you?" Zeus asked. "If you experience everything, then will you experience being evil, a tormentor, someone who eats his own children?"

Eros's slim, golden eyebrows narrowed. His mouth quirked, showing dimples, but not a smile. "I am the god of love in all forms. And love is not always about laughter and light. But love is the transcending essence that holds all things together in the end. That keeps it all from being chaos, a loss, an un-navigable mess."

"How does such a thing as love do all that?"

"Because it is the diamond pool from which life arises. Combined with will and longing, life surges. Without those components, it wilts. It cannot sustain. When it sustains, it always seeks. Seeks that which it desires. Desire itself is love. Is power. Is creation. Without it, you are not even existing. Even a breath holds some form of continuance and why? Because of love. The body does not want to give up. One more breath. One more heartbeat. All done for love, whether it is for a person or life itself. Those who take their own lives also do it for love. Most cannot see this. But love of self also means rescuing the self when the self can no longer sustain."

"So you are talking about love beyond what I have seen in the eroticism of the Erotes." Zeus was almost afraid to say this aloud. He was still uncomfortable, embarrassed even, with his terrible performance of control, his arousal that almost took down Eros's house.

"Erotic love is a by-product of physicality. It is like breathing, as natural as that. But yes, I am talking about love beyond that, part of or apart from—it does not matter. It is the underpinning of why existence happens in the first place."

The ambient light of the library cast every shelf and book and table into shades of tan, brown, and antique bronze. The edges of the oldest books and most crumpled of parchments looked like disrupted dust, or the soft down of a ragged dove. The library smelled of ancient wood, like the wind on a rustic autumn night filled with old things.

Zeus remembered hanging from his harness on nights such as those, feeling as if the wings of the empty night were surrounding him, crushing him in black darkness. But he also remembered a touch in the air of the essence of all, of being the closest he had ever known to the stars, as if he could touch them, become them. He was, in those times, the most at one with all things. He felt all knowledge and experience piled up inside him, yet still hidden as if behind a giant, metal-forged gate just waiting to rush out. To fill him up.

On those nights, he felt the love Eros spoke of in faded dusks of deepest pinks, in quivers of grave-bent leaves that crowned his hair, in the taste of spice and smoke upon the breeze, in the naked words the wind spoke that sounded like they were calling him home. The world's golden face came to him then. The mouth opened in a terrible vastness. And yet he was only curious, not afraid.

Eros's library was like that for him. He loved it.

He turned to Eros. "I will be here," he said, "until I have finished absorbing all the information I can."

Eros said, "Shall I have your bed brought in here, too?"

Zeus watched the way his eyes sparkled, almost as if in mocking. He turned away and simply replied, "Yes."

Chapter Eight

From his bed in a corner covered in rich silks and colorful tapestries, Zeus stared around the shadowed library where he had spent the last week. He had slept only a few hours, but he was not tired. Still, he lay abed. Sometimes if he was very still, his thoughts began to coalesce into ideas and his ideas formed theories. And then, finally, strategies. The silence helped him, along with generous servings of ambrosia.

He had learned much of Cronus in his studies, how he had mutilated his own father—Zeus's grandfather—cutting off his testicles and casting them into Earth's Aegean Sea. How he took Uranus's throne for his own in the Underworld, in Tartarus and all its vast, unnamed abysses.

Cronus had grown paranoid, betrayed by love, betraying love, and could see nothing but treachery around him. He had eaten his own children to prevent their inevitable betrayals. Cronus was someone who attacked first so that he would never be hurt again. Because of pain. Because of the agony of loss of love.

But for Zeus, the more he read, the more he realized it was not enough to know of love, to have read about it, to have seen it manifested in beautiful winged men in all of its forms. Or to have felt it himself, as if falling from a precipice into a great distance.

Understanding why men or gods did the things they did—whether for love or from lack of love—could not change the fact that insane actions led to tragedy.

Zeus had no experience in such things. He had not yet lived even a partial life. He thought he knew the feeling of erotic love whenever he looked at Eros. He had watched the Erotes in all their characteristics, each one slightly different in his behavior, some happier and more forward, others thoughtful, deep, even broody. But seeing all this, reading about all of it, was not enough.

What if, at his core, his father was still good in some way? That did not change the fact that Zeus must defeat him. And it did not help him at all to know that Cronus had once ruled benevolently the most awe-inspiring and idyllic existence Earth had ever known. Even Eros, in all his infinite knowledge, had said he could not help but long for a return to that time.

If Zeus must look for weakness in Cronus, it should have helped him to learn of his past. But he still had no idea how to even begin.

"Power is a burden upon fate," Eros said from behind him.

Zeus whirled. "I didn't know you were there."

"I only just arrived."

"To speak to me in riddles?" Zeus did not want to sound ungrateful, but he was tired.

"I only meant to say," Eros began, "that power is fleeting. People, including gods, hold positions of power that come and go. It doesn't last. Cronus's time is up. You simply have to make sure of that fact."

"You act as if you already know all the future."

"Not in detail. But I have oracles who stand on the cusp of time, one foot in, one foot out. Their glimpses are real prophecy not to be ignored."

"And I am a glimpse."

"Yes. A prophecy."

Zeus felt a warmth tremble from his chest to his groin. Eros wore a shimmering green chiton that fell like a waterfall to his knees. His arms were bare, his muscles flexed and golden. His wings folded flat against his back, a feather wrap. Like gracefully curved sections of silver-lined, bronze ribbon, his hair spilled just past his shoulders, glinting. His teeth flashed white as starshine when he smiled.

84

Zeus didn't want to think how he himself might appear. He had not combed his hair in days. But Eros-- Eros was magnificent.

"Take my hand. I want to show you." Eros held out his arm, palm up.

Zeus reached for him. The warmth of the touch, hand to hand, made his head spin. Eros had transported them both—or maybe just their minds?—somewhere outside the house.

He heard water pouring off the side of a cliff before he saw it. He smelled roses, lilies, but mixed with an earthier scent of dust as if it was autumn and the flowers were old.

After his vision settled, he saw a pink sky surging to blue at its zenith. He saw that they stood on a green hill and all about them were valleys entrenched in autumn colors: pumpkin, dusk, blood. It was as if the valleys were on fire, but it was only foliage turning toward winter as far as the eye could see. A spiced breeze lifted his hair and fluttered through Eros's wings. Before them on the hill stood two columns of amber-colored marble, undecorated. These two lone pillars leaned into the soft wind.

"Where is this? Not in your arboretum."

"No," Eros replied.

"Earth?"

"Not Earth. It is one of many realms of mine. This is an apex."

"A what?"

"A pinnacle of my universe. Our universe." His voice took on a monotone. "And so it rose where myths hang along the portal pillars touching the golden past."

"A poem?" Zeus asked.

"Simply words for this place which I created. Between these gold columns is a doorway, a portal. It leads to any place you desire to go. It is through here you will find Cronus before he finds you. Through here you may enter Tartarus, the deep abyss, and meet your fate."

Zeus hated the word *fate*. "And if I don't go?"

"You will run forever, if you're lucky. But know this; he will find you."

Zeus's heart surged with determination. He would not allow his father to hunt him! At the same time, fear clenched his muscles and heated his eyes.

Eros reached out and touched his left cheek with his palm. "You will succeed."

"You say this because of some oracle."

Eros's hand pressed more firmly to Zeus's face. "I say this because I know. And because I am giving you the greatest gift you can have. A gift Cronus had once, but lost."

"What?"

"Unconditional love."

"I thought you said—"

"Shh. Our erotic connection will come later. But this is truer than any of it."

His other hand touched Zeus warmly on the bare shoulder. Suddenly, Eros's wings stretched up, white and wide, overshadowing them like a canopy, the wind combing itself through all the feathers, making them glint and shine in the autumn light. He moved forward until their bodies touched, warm and hard through their silk and cotton clothing. His head leaned forward, his bright hair brushing the side of Zeus's face, his breath like honey, his green eyes glistening. Then their lips touched.

All the power that resided inside Zeus came to a head. Every part of his body tingled, thrilled, tensed. More and more, the waves of energy poured through him. A vibrancy he'd never known set him on fire. The kiss deepened. Eros's mouth opened but did not possess. He allowed Zeus to taste him as he pulled him closer.

Zeus reached around Eros's waist, encountering silk, a break in the silk, then bare skin and velvet down. He had never wanted anything more than this, not even his own freedom while hanging from a tree for his entire boyhood. If he had to go back to that just to have Eros for one night, he'd do it. He would do anything.

If he had ever thought Eros might not love him in return, now there was no question. Eros loved. And loved deeply.

*

The Erotes appeared as if from thin air. They stood at various levels on the green hill making a half-circle around Zeus and Eros.

Anteros stepped forward, his moth-wings fluttering, and handed Zeus a red, crystal chalice.

"One more drink before you go," Eros said, smiling.

"I'm going now? But—" *I am not prepared.*

"You are ready. This ambrosia is special. It will give you added strength. The oracles are in agreement. You should go now."

Zeus took the drink. It had a musty flavor, like dust, but saturated in a thin sweetness that made him crave more. He drank it all in one breath.

"Approach the portal now," Eros commanded.

Zeus glanced about him. All the Erotes stood, heads bowed, solemn. The green grass wavered in the crisp air. This was it. No preamble. Eros was smart; he hadn't given Zeus any warning. So there was no time for him to worry, anticipate, or argue.

"Think of this as one more lesson. One that you will not fail even if it feels like failure at first. Follow your instincts now, Zeus. They will heed you well."

The ambrosia went directly into his veins, giving him a pleasant burning feeling, and a sense of lightness. The taste of it lingered on his tongue, buttery and rich. A sudden heat made his muscles flex.

"You are feeling it?"

Zeus nodded. Still, he did not want to admit he was afraid.

"The portal will not harm you. It is simply like stepping through a doorway."

Zeus allowed Eros to lead him to the leaning pillars. He reached out to clasp Eros's hand one more time, and then dropped his arm. He knew he would make a fool of himself and cling if he could. He would not let himself do that.

When they reached the area between the pillars, Zeus heard a change in the wind, as a high-pitched tone reached his ears. The hum got louder as he leaned forward.

"One step more," Eros said.

Swallowing hard, Zeus said, "I will show you I can succeed. I will do this for you."

Eros's wings stretched out, glimmering white. "You do this for us all, but also for yourself."

Zeus took the final step. As his reality began to shift, he heard an echo of Eros's voice.

"Remember I love you."

Chapter Nine

He had not entered through the grand gates. Instead, the portal had brought him within Tartarus itself and deposited him in the middle of a corridor.

Remember I love you.

The words kept ringing in Zeus's mind. His chest surged with power. Confidence.

The walls of Tartarus, which looked like black rock, were slick with moisture and almost rubbery to the touch. Hot breezes blew through its halls, many accompanied by fetid odors of burnt pitch, rotted fruit, the musk of ages turned foul.

But even in Tartarus, the wonders of creativity had touched the depths. Arches of burning white adamantine framed every doorway to another hall or corridor branching into gray unknowns. Those arches gave off light. At the angle where wall and ceiling met, elaborately sculpted faces, skulls, stags, dragons, centaurs, wolves and more ran down the endless seams of a ceiling that oozed a warm slickness.

Cells lined every corridor, left to right, the thick slate doors carved in elaborate and vine-twisted designs. Some gave off such coldness as to rival an Earth winter. Others felt empty. Still others held rustles and moans. The air about the doors had the gnarled look of guttered candles. A gloss of shadows puddled the floor.

Zeus had studied Tartarus as much as he could, but it was still very much a mystery. It was a strict stronghold, a prison with rules. No one wandered about. No one made messes. No one ever escaped unless they were allowed to go free.

Occasional screams wafted through the depths of endless tunnels. Suffering and sorrow permeated its realm, but Zeus knew from his studies that Cronus did not needlessly torture the prisoners that resided there. What tortures did occur were relegated to the deepest pits, the darkest hollows, where sound did not carry, where silence meant dread. Down in those depths, Cronus had imprisoned his own father, Uranus, after taking a scythe to his testicles and emasculating him.

Zeus wondered if he himself would end up down there, cloaked in inescapable darkness, mired in original fear and sorrow, never again to know wind, light, or love. To dream only the shiver and shudder of what Eros called time in the abyss: the cold years.

He had no idea which corridor led down into the deeper pits of Tartarus. But he didn't need to. Cronus would find him. Then they would fight. And one or the other of them would end up in the pit.

Though Zeus had only just arrived, already Cronus must have sensed him.

Echoing footsteps from faraway made the walls drum.

Even a god could feel the subtle chill. The hairs on Zeus's arms and legs stood on end. The light seemed to dim. Or maybe it was only Zeus's fear. It churned up from the bottom of his stomach. He had read and learned as much as he could. He'd been told many things by Eros, by the Erotes. His expectations were for the worst.

Zeus forced himself to keep moving. One foot in front of the other. His fingertips tingled.

Drinking ambrosia for the time he was a guest in Eros's home had strengthened his power. The special ambrosia he'd drunk just before he had stepped through the portal's pillars had left Zeus with his mind spinning, his body hyped.

He had that strength to boost him. Ability. Raw talent. If, that was, he believed Eros, who believed in something called an Oracle who prophesied that Zeus would someday rule the Cosmos.

But Zeus wasn't sure if he believed. He wasn't sure of anything except his love for Eros. He wanted to prove himself. He wanted to show everyone, gods of the past and gods to come, all the beings he had never met, that he was worthy. But most of all, he wanted to show Eros that he could do this. Prove Eros right.

Oh how badly he wanted Eros to be right. But he had not had time to completely convince himself.

In his peripheral vision, Zeus saw a shadow dart across the expanse at the end of a corridor to his left. He turned abruptly. Seeing nothing, he headed in that direction. It was the only sign he'd received that anyone was down here, or might know he'd arrived.

He narrowed his brows, peering into the distance. Something moved. Dark. Wavering. No discernable shape.

Zeus's breath caught fast in his lungs. Should he call out? Obviously it had seen him. If it had eyes.

But he swallowed the urge to speak and kept silent. The shadow vanished. Only stillness filled the void of the great, long hall. All he heard now were the echoes of his own footsteps, soft and slightly scraping the black floor.

He wore the clothing he'd worn while living in Eros's library, thin, pliant leather boots, a gift from Eros. And a deep red chiton edged in gold, which the Erotes had brought him, though they themselves never wore clothing. He had no armor, not that he needed it. And no robe to get in the way of his hands and arms so as not to curb his lightning-strike gift. He could have been naked for all the protection the thin garments gave him. He could have been no one, just a prisoner himself walking the long passageway.

"I wondered when we would meet."

Zeus whirled on the voice from behind, hands slightly raised, fingers outstretched and tingling.

A man taller than Zeus himself stood before him, dark-haired with a tanned face shaped like a heart. He smiled and his white teeth flashed. He had the most unassuming stance. Bare-chested, he wore a skirt of tan leather, and sandals that fastened all the way to his knees. Even with his powerful shoulders, muscled arms and legs, and chiseled abs, Zeus sensed no threat.

"Who are you?" Zeus asked.

The man tilted his head. Fine strands of hair hung forward on his face, almost touching his eyelids. A tender smell of youth permeated the air like powder, like springtime. In such a dark environment, it was out of place.

"Do you not know it in your heart?"

Zeus frowned.

"I am from a Golden Age."

"As are many beings," Zeus replied. His body was tight with distrust, but his fear remained at a low simmer.

The man laughed. "Yes. I know. But you wound me, now."

"How?"

"You do not sense our kinship?"

Zeus felt his breath quiver in his lungs. "Cronus?" He shook his head. "It can't be."

"Ah, what did Eros tell you? That I was some evil being? Disfigured, or an ugly, tall giant with a penchant for eating babies? Did the gods send you to conquer me? Did they tell you I'm not quite sane?"

Zeus did not answer.

Cronus took a step forward. Zeus flinched, and the itch in his fingertips heightened. He backed up one step.

"But by the very gods, you are stunning, my son. Absolutely beautiful! It is a crime that Rhea hid you from me. She has quite a temper. But now you have found me and I am quite happy about that." Cronus moved forward again, graceful, soft-featured, young. His arms came up.

Zeus said, "Do not touch me."

Cronus sighed, but did not encroach further on Zeus.

"I can smell him on you."

"What?"

"Eros loves to interfere in other people's lives. Arrow to the target." Cronus lifted his hands and made a motion with thumb and forefinger curled, his other hand poking at the circle his fingers made. "Some gods are like that. Trouble-makers. Liars."

"Eros is the god of love," Zeus said.

"Yes. All forms of love. Including the love of a father for a son. But Eros has no father, and so he resents us. He and I go back a ways. He is not what he appears to be."

"He was wise and compassionate with me," said Zeus.

"Good. I want you to be well-cared for. I have no wish to see you harmed, though some might have told you otherwise."

"If this is true, then I would like to meet my brothers and sisters, for surely they are well and not existing in limbo in the belly of a Titan."

"Of course you should meet them. But they are not here. They do not live here. In fact, I am only here part of the time myself. This place takes care of itself for the most part. And its prisoners are quite secure. Would you like a tour?"

Zeus shook his head. "I would like to leave here on the assurance that you will not hunt me or harm me. That is all. I would like to end this meeting between us without any fight or animosity. Both of us winners."

"But I have no animosity toward you. These are presumptions and fictions put into your head. I revere you, Zeus, for you are my son."

Zeus thought hard on all the books he had read, all the things he had seen and heard in his very short and sheltered life. He did not have much experience, but he knew the motivations of people were all different, all personal. As far as the gods were concerned, longevity was both a luxury and a curse, for it drove many insane and seeking the memory-quench of Lethe.

Cronus had not had a dose of Lethe in millennia. In fact, no one knew how long it had been. As much as Zeus longed for the love of his father, and never to have to fight him, he could not trust the mind of this man. And yet, the same could be said of Eros. The great god of love was the oldest of them all, and had never mentioned actually imbibing the liquid of Lethe himself.

And did it make any sense at all that Zeus should confront his father alone? That Zeus could not have brought an army of gods to help him? That he must be alone in this horror of meeting his madman father?

It was the question he'd asked Eros and the Erotes over and over. *Why can't you help me?*

He'd never gotten a clear answer.

"What can I do, Zeus, to set you at ease?" Cronus asked, as if reading his mind.

Zeus did not reply.

Cronus sighed, his dark eyes wide with hope, and maybe a little mirth. He said, "I want you to feel safe and comforted. Maybe this will help." He waved his hand. He had a golden bracelet on his wrist and it flashed pink, yellow and green.

Zeus started, as if tripped, and caught his balance. He was no longer standing in a warm, moist passage of gray darkness and strange shadows. Now he was in a brightly-lit room, yet he had felt no passing of air or space. It was as if only the surroundings had changed. When Eros had teleported him, he'd felt the wind. This was… nothing.

That was when Zeus realized he was completely out-maneuvered, though this new room was ornate and beautiful, with a table set with blue and red glass pitchers and chalices. A fountain chattered in one corner. A balcony jutted off the side on which it seemed the sun shone, and flowers bloomed along the square beds and ceramic pots that lined the inner walls and the balcony railing, but it could just as easily have been a prison cell that Cronus transported them to, or even the edge of the cold abyss.

"No fears," Cronus said softly. "Are you shaking?"

Zeus shook his head, hiding his fury. "I simply don't want you to do that again."

"Of course. It is shocking for the first time. My apologies." Cronus bowed a little, his hair falling to the side of his forehead in such a youthful manner that Zeus's heart caught at the beauty of it.

"It wasn't my first time. Eros teleported me. But it was different."

"Yes. We are all different in the styles with which we comport our gifts. I like it neat and tidy and silent. Eros likes the wind in his hair."

"Where are we?" Zeus asked.

"In a place where I have attempted to recapture a bit of the Golden Age. You know what the Golden Age is, do you not?"

Zeus nodded. "When you ruled a near-perfect world. Where all beasts, humans and immortals got along, and no one ever toiled or suffered."

"It was a time words cannot quite convey. You had to be there to know and feel it. Why, your sister Hera said, just the other day, that this place is so much of a paradise for her, she never wants to leave."

"My sister is here?" Cautious, still, he did not want to get his hopes up. But if he could see her, meet her, maybe he could begin to believe Cronus just a little, and know that the stories from Eros and the predictions of the Oracle did not have to be true. People could change. Gods could come in and out of madness. Worlds could die and be re-built.

"She is."

Zeus pressed his lips tight, forcing himself to breathe slowly. It was all a trick; it had to be. And yet he so wanted to believe his father. He desperately wanted to leave him in peace, and be left in peace himself.

This young man standing before him with his long black bangs, and his sweet smile, beguiling, lacking any rage, gave Zeus hope. Naïve as it seemed, he longed for this visage of Cronus to be true. Longed with all his heart.

Cronus moved to the table and poured red liquid into two chalices. He held one out for Zeus. Zeus made no move.

"Are you not thirsty?"

Zeus shook his head.

"Ah, the trust issue. I understand. I will drink first." Cronus took the chalice he was about to hand to Zeus and put it to his lips, drinking deep. His neck flexed as he swallowed. When he was finished, he looked at Zeus, holding out the second chalice.

"I am not thirsty."

"I would not poison you. Why would I? I already have the upper hand, my son. But that's beside the point. I am not going to make a move against you. But know this. If I were going to, you would not see it coming."

Zeus balked.

Cronus laughed lightly. "Sweetheart, I wish I could have seen you growing up. You are such a delight. It is a shame you were hidden from me all these years."

Zeus's hands began to tingle again. The words were all correct and right. His father was a tall and beautiful and youthful god who appeared fair and wise. But everything was wrong. Just wrong. He could feel it in the very air itself.

Zeus said tightly, "I did miss having a father. And a mother."

"Of course you did. How were you raised? What happened in your life? I want to know these things. I want to know everything about you."

The power inside him grew. Cronus narrowed his brows. "Now, Zeus, I just offered you a drink and asked politely about your childhood and said I would not trick you. Yet you flex your power in here. To me. That is not nice. Put your lightning bolts away, my son."

The words rivered over him, causing hesitation. This was his father. Yet if he trusted Eros, his mission was a just one. And he did trust him. With his heart. Which was everything. He came to fulfill a destiny. Eros would not have lied.

He managed a quick retort. "Then let me see my sister Hera. You said she was here."

A flash of irritation crossed Cronus's pleasant features. "But of course. You need not phrase it as an order. You could have merely asked."

Zeus took a quick, hitched breath. Heat furrowed within his chest.

Cronus gave a little laugh. "You are so young. I can help with that, you know."

"What?"

"Controlling your power."

Zeus began to speak.

Cronus raised his hand to interrupt. "I mean to teach you. That is all. I can feel it welling within you, such strength. But know this, Zeus, if you wield it upon me I have the power to defend against it. And it won't be good for you."

Zeus clenched his fingers to fists. All about him the light shone. The plants smelled fresh and green. He even heard birdsong. He wanted to believe it all, let his guard down, relax. He tried to unlock his muscles, shrug his shoulders back, and ease his stance. But a spot in the center of his chest just below his heart knotted tight, a searing flame.

Cronus raised an eyebrow. "That's a little better. Maybe you should sit."

The chair Cronus indicated for Zeus appeared to be many arms carved from wood, each arm ending in a hand that grasped another hand, crossing, criss-crossing, creating the framework below a hammock of woven leather. The chair stood a few feet away from the table. Cronus took a taller, high-backed chair at the head. He stared at Zeus for a moment, and then smiled, glancing casually toward the green landscape beyond the balcony.

"I've found, in my long life, it's easier to eat sitting. But you may stand if it pleases you."

"I don't need to eat," Zeus said.

"Of course we gods do not *need* to eat. But it pleases some of us to do so. I love to eat. I have Greek delicacies in your honor, for I know you were raised in that culture."

"May I see Hera first?"

"She has already been invited. But who knows when she will arrive."

Zeus thought of Eros again, and all he'd tried to teach him. The weapons and physical combat training were useless. Cronus was too powerful. Those lessons were more about discipline and decorum. The library taught him a quiet of the mind. Forward thinking. But none of these attributes offered power.

His confidence in his destiny had never been strong. And now, here with Cronus at a whimsical dinner party, Zeus had no plan other than to keep Cronus interested, talking, calm.

Moving forward, Zeus sat in the strange chair. It felt warm against the thin fabric of his clothing, but was yielding, comfortable.

Cronus took a sip of wine, his smile still wide, his face too youthful for one so old.

"My son, you are tense and restless. What stories has Eros been filling your mind with?"

Instead of answering, Zeus decided to ask his own questions. "How do you know Eros?"

"On Earth, during the Golden Age, he visited often. He commended me for all I had done to bring about such prosperity to humans who were such a wild bunch, and still are. A violent lot. I had them tamed for millennia. And nature was in balance."

"You seem proud of that time. Can you not bring it back?"

"Everything about being immortal is about change. Change does not always involve improvement. Sometimes dark times come and stay for a while in order for change to bring future enlightenments. And so the cycle goes on and on and even I, the most powerful Titan to ever exist, cannot stop it."

"And now you rule over darkness, imprisonment."

"You say that as if it is a bad thing. Better to rule here than be imprisoned here. So some say, but it is not necessarily true. Experiencing Tartarus, many beings arrive at a fullness of being that is explosive, ecstasy unending."

Zeus knew the difference between bound and unbound. His childhood taught him that. Unbound was better, but Cronus's madness saw being bound as ecstasy? "I am not sure I understand."

"The dark and the light aren't that much different. Freedom. The cage. All just points of view. What our minds tell us is bad or good is learned opinion. Why should light—sunlight and spring—be of any more value than autumn and darkness. Both have beauty. Both give power to life, and depth. The creatures of the dark are just as beautiful as those who glow in the daylight. In Tartarus, the balance of nature remains."

"You talk as if living here is not punishment."

"No. It is punishment. But I see all sides. I choose to rule in Tartarus because I can be of help to others, those who need or even crave the dark, whose shadow souls can be made whole through breaking, re-making, which turns to longing and wonder. The creative mind blooms as much in dark as in the light."

"Or it goes mad."

"With madness comes greatness, too. I am a generous and giving god. Everything I do is for the betterment of others. I see it as a calling."

Zeus had read of prisons among the many subjects in Eros's library. "You are speaking of rehabilitation, then?"

Chuckling, Cronus replied, "So much more than that, my son. So much more."

"But your subjects are changed, you say. For their own betterment and the betterment of all as a result."

"Yes. But you are still seeing only the surface, Zeus. They become new gods, expansive, blossoming beyond what even we long-lived immortals know. It is a beginning, this imprisonment, not an end. The expansion of the soul itself."

"How?"

"You ask a question that mere words cannot answer because language is still evolving and cannot yet encompass this. Even Eros is too limited to understand, so he could not teach the truth to you about me, about my vision. But maybe you, Zeus, as my son, are powerful enough to see? Maybe you would allow me to show you?"

A burst of adrenalin coursed through Zeus, gripping his stomach, stinging every inch of his skin. He heard a drumming in his mind. He did not want to say "yes", but this was his father who walked a thin line between madness and genius. He could not say "no", either, for fear of repercussion. He gripped the sides of the chair. He thought he felt it move.

Cronus cocked an eyebrow. "You are curious, are you not?"

"I came here for one purpose, Father. To ask you—to implore you to leave me be for now. Just leave me be. I have been told all my life you would hunt me if you had any hint to my location. I've been taught to fear you. I don't want to fear you. I ask as your son, should I be made to feel this way?"

"No, you should not. But you are my son. How can you ask me to leave you alone? It is a cruelty leftover from Rhea's jealousies, no doubt. To disallow me from getting to know my own son is an attack upon my very heart."

"I understand that, but can you see my point of view? I have never known you. All I have known is that you ingest your own offspring. Even if it is a lie, that does not solve the problem of trust between us."

"But trust cannot develop if you don't allow it, Zeus."

He thought of Eros. Suspicion came even with love.

The chair beneath Zeus seemed to move again. He jerked forward, lips pressed tightly together.

"Relax," Cronus said softly. "It does not bite. Only binds."

100

Zeus tried to rise but the chair's arms curved about him, hugging itself to his legs, wrists, waist and chest. He tried to stand but the chair remained stationary, as if attached to the floor.

Panic flooded his senses.

Fire flickered through him, replacing the adrenalin from moments ago. Heat shifted up and down his legs and arms, filming his vision with a pink-orange glaze. He looked up through that flame-mist at Cronus and saw his father quietly watching, muscled arms crossed, face cold, still, stone.

His power tried to discharge but nothing happened. His insides only grew hotter. The drumming in his head became thunder. He cried out, "What have you done?"

"Allow me to explain. I am making you into a better god." Cronus's voice trembled the air with a low, cold tone.

"Let me go!" Zeus yelled.

"Oh, my son, if only it were that easy."

Zeus struggled with all his considerable strength. Neither the chair, nor the arms that comprised the chair, budged. His power sizzled inside him with no way out. It was as if it hit a wall every time he tried to lash out. He was a god on fire and there was no release.

Cronus stood and made his way to Zeus, circling the chair, reaching out every once in awhile to touch a shoulder, a cheek, a lock of dark hair. Zeus flinched every time, his gaze following his father as he walked around and around him.

He heard Eros's voice in his mind again. *To face your father is your fate.*

But what did that mean?

According to Eros, the Oracle he knew said Zeus would become the most powerful ruler of the gods. But Zeus realized the time-frame was unspecific. When would that happen? Now? In a thousand years? More?

It would seem the latter, because in this moment Zeus saw no way out of his father's grasp. A grasp Eros had led him to like a pet on a leash.

What did he have left in his arsenal? Nothing. He never had anything to win this match to begin with. Had Eros had sent him to sure failure? But to what purpose? He could not believe that. *Remember, I love you.*

"Let me go," Zeus pleaded. But there was no conviction in his voice now. No strength. Something was bleeding it all away. There had to be a purpose for this loss of power to happen, but he couldn't see it.

"I promise I will explain to you in great detail why I cannot."

Zeus bowed his head, shut his eyes. He tried to imagine himself back in the glade with Adamanthea. Or in Eros's massive home wandering the sleek corridors into room after room of artifacts, glistening pools, arboretums, the library. There was no safety for him. No sanctuary. Not anymore.

He'd never had a life to begin with. Why did he think he had anything to lose? But he thought of Eros and knew his desire for the primordial god to be unwavering. He couldn't lose that. He'd only just found that depth inside him, that ability to want what went beyond the senses and into something more.

Though his desire was unconsummated, it could not be destroyed. No matter what happened, he could take that bit of himself anywhere, live with it, and hope with it.

He raised his head and looked at Cronus dead on now.

"You can keep me, imprison me, ingest me, but it won't stop this change you talk of from happening to all of this, Tartarus, you. Eventually, your reign will end."

"You dare to talk to me about change, whelp? I've been through more change than your immature mind can even imagine. This is about you and me, my son."

"How?"

"You are mine and no one else's. That can never be changed. It is a fact. And I am stronger for having you. Don't you see?"

Zeus shook his head.

"By taking your power into me, I am more than the sum of my parts. And I plan to do just that."

He moved closer, and Zeus smelled the honey of ambrosia about him, but deeper, beyond that sweet layer, was an underlying scent of salt and burning and ash, as when autumn turns and approaches winter with an unruly but beautiful form of destruction. Simply, Cronus smelled old. Very old.

Unlike the oldness of Eros, this man exuded a kind of rage, maybe even unchecked sadness that led to deeper anguish, and Zeus turned his head away, not understanding, unsure how to respond.

Cronus bent closer to Zeus now, his breath touching him, hot and possessing. The fine hairs on Zeus's arms rose.

Zeus struggled, but the chair held tight. His sandals slapped the floor. He turned his head further away, but nothing stopped Cronus from coming closer and closer.

"Please!" Zeus yelled.

Lips touched his neck. Warm and yielding. Zeus tossed his head. The kiss was not the kiss of affection, it was tight and pushing and controlling. Then he felt a pinch as if a sharp object stabbed him. Warmth from breath and his own blood singed his skin. Pain stung him in a sudden blow. He cried out again and again. His voice echoed through the sunlight, across the food-laden table, bouncing against the clean, white walls.

Everything went black.

Chapter Ten

He woke in darkness. He felt no pain. If he had sustained an injury to his neck from Cronus's bite, he had healed. At least he had that god-trait for comfort.

Gradually, his vision cleared as his eyes got used to the shadowy surroundings. He could see he was in a dim room. He was standing upright, held tight by chains about his body, arms, and legs. He could not move. He could not fall. His back pressed against spongy warmth.

Zeus looked at down the chains. About as thick as his middle finger, they appeared too weak to restrain him. But when he tried to pull free they held fast.

A door opened. Cronus entered. He wore a dark tunic, and over that a black cloak that shifted behind him like wings.

Zeus coughed, but said nothing. Cronus spoke not a word, but went about the room waving his hand, making soft glowing light emit from the walls. With another wave, a table appeared. On it were metal tools, like cutlery, and two bowls. One bowl streamed fine lines of smoke, acrid, like burning hair.

He looked at his father through the smoke and shadows and flickering light—all part of the scene set to make this Tartarus chamber more shadowed and eerie. Intimidation worked on the weak. But Zeus did not feel weak. He felt fine and strong. Simply, he could not move.

Betrayal settled through him in a burning outrage. He waited for it to fill and burn through his veins, for his power to grow. The lightning inside answered to fury more than sweet talk. Eros had told him this. It was the youth in Zeus, the uncontrolled shudder of new power. Every god went through a process of power and gifts being ruled more by anger and despair than moments of complacency and comfort. Pleasure was another matter.

But Zeus felt no pleasure in this moment.

The flames inside him began to lick. His predicament ensnared his sanity. But instead of rushing forth, the fires inside him spat small sparks at his finger-tips and then subsided, as they had when he was imprisoned by the strange chair.

Turning, Cronus said, "Why Zeus, were you thinking you might aim your beautiful gift at me again? And worse, that I would not take further precautions against that?"

Zeus shook the fog from his head, confused.

Cronus's predatory, dark eyes gazed through the smoke of weak sizzles that still tried to break free of Zeus's hands. The incense swirled up: spices of burnt sourness that made him want to gag.

"You are bound by titanium. As a Titan, the metal is your ally, unless another Titan uses it against you. I have enhanced the links with small, minute force fields. You cannot break them. And your fires, ah, your beautiful fires are contained. It is like an invisible cage. Tartarus is full of them. Did Eros not teach you this?"

The technology of the gods, beyond individual powers each god might be born with, was not something to grasp in a couple of weeks. Zeus had little insight into things called "force fields" and therefore no idea how to navigate through them. Like breaking a spell. One needed another spell. He had no clue how he might attain that.

At the mercy of Cronus, he must focus on what was at hand. His pathetic childhood spent hanging from a tree, and Eros's lessons had taught him to think. At the very least, he had a creative mind.

But fear staunched creativity, and his body quivered against the warm rock at his back; the chains themselves were ice against his bare skin. He realized only then he was naked. His red chiton was gone. His sandals.

His mind kept scrambling to take it all in, imagining in flashes a dozen horrific scenarios of Cronus eating him, bit by bit, as Zeus, who could not die, watched himself be taken apart.

Cronus had already bitten him. Before Zeus had passed out, he'd felt the old god suck the very blood from the vein in neck.

Moans built up in the back of his throat.

Focus.

The voice in his mind sounded like Eros.

He tried to hear it again, but it did not return.

He tried not to panic further as he watched Cronus motion with his hand. Two dark-cowled beings entered and set the table. They brought trays with more utensils, and spread them out, along with a chalice, a pitcher, and some golden plates. They seemed not to have the magic of Cronus, and manually lit candles that they placed in fancy, black candelabras and set about the chamber to flicker demon-shadows across the gray walls.

How could someone delight in all this?

A monster. Yet Cronus stood in the center of it all, the bustle of the scene, the glimmering horror, a shining beauty. Zeus had to marvel at his grace and comeliness. He would have passed for a youth if you didn't look closely at his eyes, or the tight, glib almost-smile of his full and pouting lips.

A boy so old he had lost his mind.

In the surreal gloom, Cronus made a wide-sweeping gesture with his arm. A group of minstrels dressed in black entered. Zeus had never seen minstrels, but he knew what they were. He knew about music, if in theory only.

They wore strange red cowls and masks made of bone. Their cloaks were braided with black and silver strings of cottons and silks.

Would they play their songs for Cronus as Zeus was slowly eaten?

His body chilled. The fires in him wanted to explode outward, steam and flicker from his skin, but all they could manage were tiny sparks that cooled as soon as they emerged.

Cronus's servants pushed back their cloaks and hoods, dropping them to the floor. They stood as naked as Zeus now, and looked human, but were all beautiful, unflawed, and Zeus knew they were gods by that alone.

He could see that chains bound them as much as they bound Zeus, just looser, allowing them the ability to walk freely but not escape, and not use the powers they may have been born with. These had to be gods forced into punishment in the dark underworld for deeds Zeus could not imagine.

Think.

The voice came from Zeus's head again. Soft and golden, yet firm. Almost fierce.

Zeus dropped his chin, closed his eyes. Maybe one of these servants, chained although able to move freely, might be an ally? But who would risk further torture to help a strange god who had already failed in his task to imprison Cronus the moment he'd set foot in Tartarus?

Zeus, as a stranger, offered no inspiration to them. An unknown. A baby god. A fool. Who might risk their own momentary reprieve from torture to betray Cronus under Cronus's own gaze?

No one.

His mind brought to him an image of Eros standing half-naked against a backdrop of green and gold. The arboretum. Eros's skin was blinding, glowing, the lithe muscles flexing. Eros tilted his head until his sun-fired hair streamed in a halo about him. His wings lifted behind him, white like a mist. Ethereal and light and intensely comforting.

Zeus wanted that presence, that awe. But only darkness supped at his flesh now. Cronus was already taking mental bites of him by making Zeus wait in fear, cower at what his imagination might conjure.

And Eros. Well, Eros with all that power had insisted he could not transcend to Tartarus. But now Zeus felt that must be impossible. Eros was a primordial. He could do anything, go anywhere.

Eros had left him, and at this realization Zeus lifted his head up and held back a howl.

Eros had left him.

"You have to do this yourself. The Oracle has spoken. You are to face your father alone," Eros had said.

Everything was wrong on so many levels. If gods had free will and immense power, why would they obey any rules, let alone a distant Oracle's prophecy?

Zeus blinked through his watery vision, watching the servants move about the room, the minstrels setting up, and Cronus standing like a spoiled boy awaiting the offerings of delectable gifts.

That is my father, was all Zeus could think. *That is he who made me, who is blood of my blood, skin of my skin.*

Cronus stood with his arms crossed over his chest, cloakless now, clad in a blue chiton that fell to his upper thighs, and sandals that wrapped to his knees. His dark, muscular body gave off a supernatural power, the way Eros's did. An old god. Old as the sky.

Why was this happening? But then again, what were gods if not monsters that grew old and insane?

Cronus's gaze raked Zeus now. He walked over to him, a shadow of insanity combined with an inner glow of beauty.

"What troubling thoughts are you having, my son?"

Zeus took a breath; his chains jangled. He steadied himself the best he could, and answered. "That I am your son and that I deserve more than this from you."

"Did you think it my duty to give you anything? Just because you spit from my loins?"

Zeus tried to suppress the emotional pain that shot through him, and frowned.

"I don't know. Just that if I am yours—" He swallowed.

Cronus reached out and pressed a warm palm to Zeus's forehead, fingertips weaving into his hair. "You are mine. And that is why you are here."

Zeus shook his head to try to get Cronus to stop touching him.

"And it is why you are chained to the wall."

"Is that why you drank my blood?"

"In part. I took one drop only as a test. You passed. The elixir of you is quite fine, powerful."

"Gods who drink other gods' blood. I have not heard of that."

"You are young yet," Cronus replied. "I'm sure there are many things you have not heard of."

Though it was useless, Zeus could not stop straining against the chains. The hard, smooth wall at his back grew warmer against his bare skin. The air of the room felt clammy; the shadows from the low light flickered brown and strange.

Cronus moved away from Zeus, turned to the table and picked up an oddly curved knife. It was the color of fire, a deep coppery red. In his free hand, Cronus lifted a golden goblet. Then he was back at Zeus's side, and watched him flinch.

Zeus followed the path of the miniature scythe, the sweat on his skin growing cold. Cronus had castrated his own father, Uranus. At the thought, Zeus's balls drew up tight. Suddenly, he couldn't breathe.

Gods could not die. Gods could heal, but pain was real for them, and growing new parts took time. A young panic suffused him. He blinked back tears.

Cronus touched the scythe to Zeus's jaw delicately, scraping just a little. "This won't hurt much," he said softly. "My dear, youngest son, you are so beautiful. How can I resist you?"

"What? What are you going to do?"

"This." He moved the scythe quickly down the jaw and across Zeus's throat. Zeus felt a sting followed by the warmth of spilling blood. He gasped as Cronus held the goblet up, catching the flow. Though he could not see his own wound, Zeus heard the dripping of liquid as it hit the gold sides of the cup.

He shut his eyes hard, and then opened them. A mix of emotions scrambled his brain. Horror. Rage. The keen pain of helpless despair. He had never felt this alone, even hanging from his pathetic hemp prison on Earth.

He felt betrayed in every way. By family. By new friends. Eros, even. Surely Eros had known the details of what he was sending Zeus to endure. Why did it have to done in this manner?

Zeus turned his head when a servant walked in with a floating device that looked like a box with tubes. He steered it toward Cronus. When the box was floating level with Zeus's head, Cronus took a long metal tube with a thin needle on the end and pressed it to Zeus wound.

Zeus cried out. It felt as if his neck was being ripped apart.

"Gods heal so fast, I need to keep your skin open to drain you as fast as you remake your own blood."

His stomach turned over at the words. His head spun. Cronus was going to drain him? Forever? What would that mean? He wouldn't die, but maybe it would be worse than death. To have no strength, no ability while his blood continued to rebuild itself in his system on and on, never fully completing the task.

Finally, Cronus stepped away, smiling, his dark eyes sparking with friendliness that belied his actions. "Very good, my son. This will all work out so well."

Zeus struggled to speak. "Are you going to keep me this way forever?"

"Well, at least until I have had enough." The goblet in Cronus's hand was full, the liquid at the rim shining red. "But I warn you, my appetite is massive." He took a shallow sip, not more than a drop. When he drew away the goblet, his lips glistened red.

"My, this is sweet. Young god-blood. I could become addicted to you, Zeus. I will save the rest for the big party. I wouldn't want to spoil myself too soon on your deliciousness."

Zeus wanted to beg, to scream. But his body was frozen in horror. All that escaped his throat was a swollen sob.

Eros, why?

Cronus smiled, leaned toward Zeus and kissed him lightly on the cheek. "My beloved son, I know Eros hid you these past weeks. But who hid you from me for your first 18 years? I would like to know."

Zeus knew Cronus would torture and imprison Adamanthea if he knew. He shook his head.

Cronus ran a hand down Zeus's shoulder and arm, caressing. The hand moved to his chest, his abdomen. It brushed over his genitals.

"My sweet boy. How beautiful you are. Just tell me, and I will make you more comfortable. Yes?"

Zeus flinched twice. His lightning tried to surge again, only to die, the fires inside him growing colder.

Cronus stroked his thigh and up the back of it leading up to cup Zeus's buttock. "You can't best me. You came alone because of hubris. Pride always causes failure in the young. Didn't Eros teach you that?"

Zeus tried not to whimper, but a strange sound came from inside him.

"Did Eros also fail to tell you he and I are not enemies? He's fickle that way, always has been since the beginning. Did he tell you he could not come here himself? He lies, of course. Any god can set foot in Tartarus. You are only beginning to learn what it is to be a god, Zeus."

"But why?" Zeus croaked out the words. The ache in his neck increased.

"Eros is the god of love, as you know. He cannot resist giving anyone what they want for the asking. All I had to do was ask for you. And he delivered."

Zeus shivered. Cronus was lying. He had to be lying!

And yet, though Eros had given him the special red ambrosia he said would increase his power, it had done nothing for him. For here he was, imprisoned so quickly, so easily.

Cronus motioned toward the minstrels, who began to play a tune so lovely it seemed unfitting for this new, darker place, this dining room of supping on the blood of living things.

One of the minstrels, hooded and shadowy, began to sing in a voice like water trickling through shining rocks. The words came over Zeus in a kind of beauty that made him even more uncomfortable. Some of the phrases were drowned out by Zeus's own pounding heart, but he heard:

> *The wine of golden pasts*
> *Every summer meadow covered in stardust*
> *Dusk the color of honey*
> *Goat-men kissing*

This was a nightmare. Surely he would wake, and Eros would be by his side offering solace, helping him to see who he was meant to become.

As if reading his thoughts, Cronus said, "Eros wounds with his arrows of love. That is his nature, Zeus. You fell under his arrow. He made promises to you. I understand how such a delectable virgin god of only eighteen would believe him."

Zeus opened his mouth. A yell echoed off the chamber walls, pushing past the minstrel's song. "Noooo!'

Cronus patted him on the rump, leaned in until Zeus could smell the dusting of flowers on his skin, and a strange, springtime warmth completely at odds with the atmosphere of Tartarus, of blood-drinking and torture. Cronus smelled new, not old. Fresh, not rotten. Yet surely his insides must be made of putrefaction.

Cronus brought his face very close to Zeus's, as if to kiss him again. His mouth opened and Zeus thought he saw a yawning blackness within that went deeper than the stars themselves. A pink tongue, matching the full pink lips surrounding that black hole, darted out and touched Zeus's cheek with a series of quick licks.

Zeus's mind closed in on itself. He heard the rush of his own blood as it drained. And faraway, the frantic screams of some other unfortunate prisoner. He wondered who it might be, why they were being punished, until he realized the screaming was his own, his lungs heaving, his mind squeezing in on itself, and the fire that was his essence quenched at last, frigid, ash.

Chapter Eleven

A flute-wind. Sweat on his brow. Stone against his back.

Zeus opened his eyes. Still chained against a slick wall, he observed the room around him had changed. The silvery walls were peppered with black stains. A low, hot wind blew through the nearly empty chamber, steamy, edged with the acrid scent of something dusty and old burning up. It made a sound like music, a beautiful wail of lament and longing.

He saw the black blood-box floating by his head, the strange tube still connected to his throat. It emitted a gentle whir. Had he been moved, or had everything and everyone been removed from the room?

As he tried to move his head to look right and left, dizziness overtook him. For a long while, the room whirled about him, making him sick. He closed his eyes but that only made the sickness inside him worsen.

When he looked again, the room's steamy air swirled. Something seemed to move within it. A hand, five-fingered, human-looking, waved at him. It was surrounded in whiteness as if disconnected from its source. Then another hand joined it, also waving.

The hands were reddish in coloring, unadorned. Very quickly, three more hands joined the other, then four, then too many to count. The whiteness undulated, and seemed to be made of hands. Dozens and dozens of them, as if before him stood a being made of hands, a monster.

Zeus blinked. It had to be delirium from loss of blood. All his strength was gone. It stood to reason that his strength of mind had left him as well.

Hi, my name is Chires. Hecatonchires, actually. But Chires is what they call me.

The voice did not emanate audibly. Instead, Zeus heard it in his mind like bells chiming and forming words. The words were accompanied by soft pink and yellow flashes, like petals snowing the air. The flower petals of light drifted toward him and when they met his skin they vanished. Zeus felt a tender warmth where each one touched him before it disappeared.

He opened his mouth to speak but only air came, his voice lost. He tried again and managed a whisper. "I am Zeus."

I know. Whispering bells, more pink-gold flashes.

"Are you a prisoner here?"

I am. I cannot say for how long but it feels like forever.

"I can't quite see you right. It seems you have a lot of hands."

You are right. I have 100 hands. I am made of hands.

"I don't understand."

I am a monster. I have no head or eyes or mouth. I am all hands. And so I am imprisoned.

"But why?"

I cannot remember why. I must be a very very bad monster.

"Are you chained as well?"

Yes. Tight to the wall so I can only wave but not undulate freely within my cloud for motion.

"Your voice sounds like bells falling through the air."

Does it? How nice. I cannot see as you do, of course. But with my mind I can sense the reality I am within and form visions of all that is around me. I "see" you as a beautiful, young humanoid male. You appear to me as a dark glowing silhouette with two hands only, and two legs and a head.

"I see your hands and a shimmering fog."

All of that is part of me, my mind, my form, my spirit. The hands are what are physical to your perception. Is it shocking and terrible for you?

"No," said Zeus. "Nor is being imprisoned. I've known freedom very little in my life."

115

I am sorry to hear that. It seems we share the same fate.

"We share the fate that Cronus has forced upon us."

Cronus? Ah yes, my half-brother. He always had control issues, especially with blood relatives. He has been a hero and a villain many times over in this endless life. Sometimes I have been able to see through his mind, feel light and wind upon my form. He does not like it, though. If he senses my thoughts within his, he commands Tartarus to fill my cloud with delirium vapors. Then my thoughts are only dreams. And I sleep.

The horror of this creature's existence was a nightmare not unlike Zeus's. Zeus still wondered if he was dreaming it all. Chires. His half-uncle. Trapped here for centuries, perhaps, drugged to endure it.

"Cronus is draining me of my blood as quickly as my body re-makes it. He is collecting it like wine for himself."

Yes, Cronus eats all his children. It is his way. The air sparkled as Chires's words came into Zeus's mind.

"And no one has ever tried to stop him?"

Oh, many have tried. They are all imprisoned here now.

"Eros sent me to this fate."

Eros sent you?

The sparkles on the air turned to dark specks. Zeus felt a chill. "You seem surprised."

Eros and the abyss became friends after a long and twisted battle.

"The abyss?"

The abyss is a living being. Its name is Tartarus.

"This prison is alive?"

Yes. He would not send you here unless he wanted you to suffer. Or unless he has been in communication with Tartarus to see you do your own battle and bring you safely to the other side.

"I was told I was destined to fight Cronus. But I can't do a thing. I can't move. All my strength is gone."

I understand. The color of Chires's cloud turned reddish, edged in black. The already dim chamber took on a greater darkness, though Zeus could still see the slick walls, the hard floor, and Chires's hands, now pink in color, moving all about in the undulating fog.

"You may understand, but I do not," Zeus replied. "And as for Tartarus, obviously Cronus has control over it or him, too. The entire place is under his command."

You are correct. My brother and the abyss have much in common. And Tartarus is very loyal to those it comes to love. But Eros and Tartarus go back further than Cronus's lifespan.

"Eros told me cannot come here because of Cronus's control over Tartarus. Was he lying?"

He might have lied to you, or he might have told you the truth. The nature of the abyss is always changing. Cronus rules now, yes. Perhaps the truth is that a condition of that rule is an organic rejection of Eros, should he ever try to set one wing within this structure, this body.

Zeus closed his eyes. Heat pressed the lids. "Then there is no hope."

I dream of hope.

The blood box vibrated gently, but Zeus still felt its pressure, its sting. He did not reply to Chires's statement.

After awhile, he tried to sleep but could not. The loss of blood made him dizzy and sick, but not enough to cause him to pass out. Perhaps Cronus had turned the machine on a lower setting. To make him aware. To make him suffer.

*

He did not see Cronus for a long time. He had no idea how long, but it seemed an eternity to him. Even hanging from his hemp harness for eighteen years had not been so tedious or arduous.

Chires had been silent since they'd first met, though Zeus had tried many times to talk to him again. Zeus could see the strangely moving hands in the fog, sometimes purple, sometimes red, sometimes turning white as snow and disappearing into the fog entirely. His uncle was no doubt floating in a dream-haze. Nothing sparked the air. No voiceless thoughts, no bells falling.

Zeus hung from his chains and watched the walls spin.

As he watched the tilting walls for hours, days, weeks, a moment came when light plunged the room into a white candescence. One of the walls had opened. When Zeus's eyes adjusted, he could see a bluish edge around the light, and he heard the faint sound of music. A silhouette of a man appeared in the light. He identified him through his voice before he saw him in his blood-drained haze.

Cronus.

"Zeus, you are looking well," said the voice of his father.

Zeus could only shake his head as the room twirled. If not for the chains, he would have fallen. Most of his life he'd spent hanging, never able to lie down, but now he longed to lie flat.

"And Chires. Wake up. Don't you wish to greet me?"

On the edge of his thoughts, Zeus heard Chires say sleepily, *Cronus?*

The fog of his uncle turned dark with what looked like rain.

When Zeus's vision cleared, he saw his father looking much the same as before, young with dark, glossy hair, wearing a long white tunic belted with a golden rope. His sandals crisscrossed over his muscled, tanned calves all the way to his knees.

Cronus said, "Chires, you are quite a sight." It did not seem like a compliment.

As are you, brother.

"At least I have legs and a head."

Zeus heard bells and birdsong. Was Chires laughing?

"Zeus, my beautiful boy," Cronus began. "I have collected so much blood from you and have imbibed none but that first drop from your neck, and another drop from the golden chalice you filled for me. I've been saving it for a special occasion. Now that day has come. I've decided to throw a party."

He waved his hand. Suddenly, the room became a high-ceilinged hall packed with couches, banquet tables, and people in various ornate costumes glittering with jewels. Some had horns, wings or masks. The music Zeus had heard earlier came from a group of musicians in one corner all dressed in red. They played instruments Zeus could not identify. One instrument was an upright box of levers all in a row that emitted clunky tones as the fingers pressed them.

Chained and naked, Zeus watched the partiers turn to stare at him. He was held to the center of the wall like a spectacle. People came forward to get a closer look. Since Eros had taught Zeus how to take foreign words and open his mind to the language in a moment, he understood every comment they made in their many dialects.

"They were not lying. He is the most beautiful of Cronus's offspring."

"And the biggest."

"Such deep eyes."

"The muscles are pronounced but graceful."

"What a lovely cock."

Zeus did not enjoy the compliments. Instead, he had an urge to roar and destroy. For here he was, un-free, trussed in chains before them all with a blood box continually draining his very life-essence straight from its source at the side of his neck.

Here he was, a supposedly great god betrayed by all: Eros, Cronus, Tartarus, the Erotes, and every single person at this so-called party.

More people came over to look at him. "I can't wait to taste his delicious god-blood."

"I'd like to taste more than his blood." Several people nearby snickered.

Zeus wondered what they all thought of Chires, though as he looked about the room he could not see him any longer. Chires had been left behind.

More people came up to Zeus, talking about him, commenting on his body as if he weren't there.

"Go away," he murmured under his breath. "Go away."

His words only made the spectators laugh.

So many different beings comprised the crowd. Every time he saw a winged man, his heart jumped and made him dizzier. He kept thinking it might be Eros, or his lovely winged harem boys, the Erotes, come to take him home. Wherever home was.

But of course even if one of them had been the god of love, Eros had betrayed Zeus. Neither he nor his amoretti would be here for a rescue.

"The flask of our wine is lovely tonight."

Cronus's voice rose over the chatter, loud and clear. Everyone quieted. The room's marble sculptures and finely laid tables with cutlery of gold and plates of silver glass, twinkled in the false sunlight. But all was a sham. Fake. A set. For Zeus could not see any land beyond the blue skies of the arches.

But it was well done. Scents of wild forests and sun-lit rivers blew through the warmth of the giant hall. But for Zeus, the wind was full of shivers.

"My son Zeus and I have finally been reunited after eighteen years. And you all must agree with me that he is no doubt the loveliest of my children."

The guests nodded while politely applauding.

"I have called you all here to share in my bounty," Cronus continued. "In the tradition of the olden days when gods were still young and finding their way, I now offer the blood of my son as a sacrificial drink. The old traditions formed us. Back then, the blood of the gods was mixed and shared. From it came the ambrosia that keeps us young and strong. But now ambrosia is synthesized. And the greater connection between us all has faded. So today I offer the blood of Zeus. From it, we will all be strengthened, for his is a vintage of the new age, of youth and innocence, of beauty and aspiring greatness."

120

Naked humanoid servants, both male and female, each more delicate and lovely than the last, moved about the fancy gods with clear glass pitchers filled to the brims with ruby liquid.

Zeus realized all these pitchers contained his blood, blood that had been sucked from his body as fast as he could produce it. The machine was still attached to his neck. It never stopped whirring. His blood drained into it and was transported elsewhere by means Zeus could not see or perceive.

Quickly, jeweled chalices all over the room glistened with Zeus's blood, their rims glowing red.

When everyone was served, Cronus held his chalice, the biggest and shiniest, high above his head. "I give you my son. May he reign forever in our hearts, our minds, our veins."

A cheer went up. The crowd raised their chalices. "To Zeus!"

In his dizzying vision, Zeus watched them all drain their goblets and chalices. The old familiar fire inside him began a low glow, a feeling he hadn't had in a long time. It started to lick about his chest and arms, but just as he thought it might get a hold within him and spread throughout his body, it fizzled.

He moaned softly. His head fell forward, his dark hair swinging along the sides of his cheeks. As the crowd drank, he could feel the diminishing of his entire being.

Eyes closed, body hanging limp in his chains against the wall, naked and trapped, he listened to the clinking of metal against metal as people toasted one another, heard the slurps and gulps of greedy mouths as they had second and third helpings of him. They were celebrating his captivity. Having an orgy with the essence of his being.

Zeus's mind floated. He focused away from the clamor and onto his swirling thoughts. He watched the darkness behind his closed eyelids, and tried to drift away. He did not want to be conscious any longer. He did not even want to be alive. But he could not die.

Somewhere deep inside him, he felt a breaking, a letting go. Chires had said he still dreamed of hope. Zeus had no idea what a dream like that even looked like. He had never felt it as a youngster, and he did not feel it now. Whatever it might be, Zeus was bereft of the experience.

A yawning darkness opened inside him. He remembered Eros telling him of it; he had a strength of darkness within him that he needed to be aware of, for within it raged all manner of terrible things: resentment, hatred, anger and the heat of outrage.

Self-pity sizzled in a pale rain that smelled sharply of tears. A black shadow encroached, filled with an emptiness that promised no pain, no suffering, no feeling, but asked for his soul in return. Every memory the shadow touched hardened, then broke into jagged pieces that became non-linear, out of context.

He saw Adamanthea. The boys in the glade Zeus had unintentionally killed. Books. Seasons. The arrival of the Erotes. Soft caresses. New knowledge. Desire sweeping him into unchecked longing. Glimpses of what he thought might be love for Eros. All of it became meaningless to him, as if it had happened to someone else he would never relate to.

The shadow gave him a weird solace. He didn't care about anything anymore. He wanted to laugh at all these gods. At Cronus. Wanted to shout, "Do your worst!" and curse them all. It was easy now to embrace it all, and let it fall away like shudders and leaves in the wind.

The shadow promised him this management of himself. This control. Unnatural. Natural. It was a way out of the maze he now found himself in, but he had to go dark and deep to find that door out.

He wanted it. He went willingly, diving into the ink of endless night which came up to swell around his nearly numb mind. But as soon as he jumped into the deepening blackness, a sound distracted him. Like a distant storm. A choking of air. An exhale of astonishment.

The blackness spun its solid web, but for one last glimpse of light, Zeus opened his eyes a crack. Blurred images of fallen people, their bodies unmoving, littered the floor. They were not dead. They blinked. They breathed, but they did not move.

Zeus opened his eyes wider, peering across the vast hall. Some gods remained standing, but stumbling. Others caught themselves against tables or chairs, trying to balance, retching, spitting red from their slick and trembling mouths. Many more fell with loud thunks to the floor, twitching, then growing still.

The room had become mostly quiet. The false light had dimmed.

The shadow hovered in Zeus's mind. Steel. Cold. Zeus ignored it as he searched the room for his father. Then he saw him, red staining his white tunic, mouth a slashing grimace. Cronus still stood, though. The last. The oldest. And would not fall. His dark eyes raked over Zeus. Darker than the shadow beckoning within. Darker than anything Zeus had ever known.

"You!" Cronus said, tone even, almost soft. It carried across the silence like a yell. A challenge. A weapon.

Zeus's chains rattled.

Cronus moved slowly, steps uneven, unbalanced, but he could still walk. He took up a knife from a plate of roasted fowl, and lurched like a drunk toward Zeus.

"You," he said again, teeth gritted.

Zeus tried to take a step back, but could not move. Cronus nearly fell against him, knife up-raised, and though he was weak, the knife was sharp, and it plunged over and over again into Zeus's chest and belly. Cutting him. Stripping the skin from his bone.

Zeus howled. The jump he'd made was still happening. Darkness crooned to him, beckoned. The pain drew the shadow closer about him, a cloak of chill, of astonished anguish turned hollow, trustless. He whimpered once.

The machine at Zeus's neck fell away, crashing to the hard floor, breaking into three pieces. His neck healed almost instantly, but the cuts to his body, though dry from lack of blood, were painful and deep.

Cronus stopped stabbing as he fell to his knees, then onto his side. He could no longer stand. The knife fell, clattering.

The walls behind Zeus moved. The chains fell.

Chapter Twelve

Shaking a little. Now free. Zeus stood, naked, looking down at his father.

Pain wracked him, and he held his hands over his stomach, trying to hug himself back to wholeness. He usually did not feel pain, but this hurt him. Maybe it was because Cronus had done it. The stab wounds went deep on levels more than just physical. Part of him wanted to crawl away forever, see no one, and lick his wounds.

For a long time he stared at the helpless body of Cronus, still alive, eyes open and watching him, his dark hair spilling across the white floor, his strong muscles contracting but unable to budge his limbs.

All across the banquet hall the bodies of gods lay, some heaped upon one another, a strange scene of cultish carnage. The only beings still standing were a few naked servants, most of who were fleeing through doorways to rooms unseen. They were human, powerless; Zeus did not care about them.

The shadow within him made him feel apart from all of it. As if it was happening to someone else. He found his voice and it came up from his lungs in an icy breath.

"It seems, Father, you have lost all your power here."

Zeus could not explain it at all, but obviously it had something to do with his blood. He never saw it coming. Obviously, neither had Cronus.

Zeus laughed at his own thought. Already his stomach and chest were healing and he felt a little better, except for the shadow about him, and a need for further justice.

The shadow made him dizzy. His rage became edged with a slice of grief that felt as if it were cutting through his lungs and heart.

"Now it's my turn," Zeus said. He kicked at the limp form of Cronus, then raised his head and called for the servants to return.

"Come back, servants! I will not hurt you." *Yet.*

That was when he saw Eros, white wings backlit in gold in the waning light. At the sight of the winged god, his dizziness returned, but different. Eros's beauty outshone everything about him. Blond waves of hair rested against broad shoulders. Topaz armbands circled his upper arms, the muscles firm but graceful. Eros wore a scintillating, nearly transparent, leaf-green robe belted with braided, gold rope. The garment was sleeveless and swept the floor in a liquid ripple. His wide green eyes caught an edge of noontime glow, glistening. His high cheekbones and smooth, square jaw made all thoughts within Zeus stop.

Before Zeus could blink, Eros moved with god-speed to his side and caught him under the arms. Zeus had not realized he was already falling until his cheek and temple butted Eros's chest. Where did this weakness come from? He was stronger now, unchained. He was healing.

He yearned still for Eros, but he did not want the god's touch, and tried to push him back.

"It's all right. You won. Tartarus answers to you now, which is why your chains fell."

"You betrayed me," Zeus whispered. Then he repeated the words, eyes closing, and saw the darkness at the edges of his inner vision begin to close in again.

"You were never, for one moment, forgotten. My awareness was on you since you entered the abyss."

"You knew my father would capture me. Torture me." His voice broke and he lost touch with all but the bleak dark growing around him. It comforted him. It seduced him with a

126

feeling that Eros was nothing compared to its encompassing hollows.

"Hush," said Eros. "I'm taking you home."

He felt the warmth of a flush on his face when he said, "I don't want to go with you."

As if he did not hear him, Eros picked him up, even as large as Zeus was, and cradled him like a baby. Zeus felt the god's breath against his ear.

"You need rest. Cronus—all of them—will sleep now from the effects of your blood. Tartarus will deal with them."

The effects of his blood? What had Eros done to him?

Despite his pain and his anger at Eros, his body curled into the golden chest. Physically, he still wanted Eros. It was readily apparent. But this being had sent him to his torment with little warning, and no hope, keeping secrets, using Zeus and his blood as bait. There was no reconciliation in his mind for a man who could do that to him, no matter how accommodating and enticing Eros was. No matter that Zeus had fallen in love.

He did not want explanations. He only wanted to take his revenge on Cronus and all his cohorts. And he wanted to keep control of Tartarus, if indeed it was true that Tartarus answered to him, now, and put anyone who harmed or threatened him in its deepest pits forever. Even Eros.

But no, he couldn't do that. He wouldn't, no matter how cloying his internal darkness became.

His entire body shuddered at the thought, and Eros only held him closer, whispering more words. "You're safe now. You will sleep and then we will talk."

Zeus felt softness encompass him. He was still so weak. He did not want to open his eyes. His mind fell. In an echoing distance, the shadow darkness swept through him, as if to hold him tight in mind the way Eros held him in body.

Then he heard a mind-voice, not Chires, but someone else who communicated in the same style.

I am Tartarus.

Zeus glimpsed a vast network of mazes and alleys, a world of avenues like fingers reaching ever further into the unknown.

I will form and meet and trap at your command.

A black silhouette of a man appeared behind Zeus's closed eyelids, lean and tall. Stars glittered within his frame as he raised one hand, turning it palm up, and placed it against his waist. He bowed.

Before Zeus could react, sleep caught him in her starry net.

*

Anteros slipped naked from the sapphire pool. He stood over Zeus, tanned and handsome, dripping cool water onto him. Zeus lay on a cushioned lounge, staring up at latticework that revealed stars beyond a glass roof.

Over and over, he kept seeing the silhouetted star man that was Tartarus bow. He turned away, wordless, from Anteros's rain. He was still weak, having only awakened an hour ago here in Eros's abode in his own huge, pillow-stocked bed.

It figured that Eros was nowhere in sight when he awoke. The pain of that sliced through his chest. He'd wandered through the halls until he came into the pool room with its new roof—Zeus had demolished the old one—and its vista of stars.

He'd already had three servings of ambrosia, but his shakiness remained.

All he wanted was to return to Tartarus and see to Cronus's incarceration himself. As long as he could stand, he could command the servants there, take charge. Eros had said as much. Tartarus answered to Zeus now. He'd heard him in his mind.

A sudden light folded upon the air with the scent of sun beating on rivers, and honey on the lips. Zeus pulled his knees up, his chiton riding high on his thighs, the single fastening at his left shoulder pulling tight. His heart began again to hurt.

Eros stood before him, nearly blinding.

Zeus resented that he could not apparate like that, and wondered if he'd ever be able to. Otherwise, he'd be in Tartarus right now.

Anteros said, voice far too bright and shiny for recent events, "Good morning!"

"Leave us," Eros said.

Zeus sat up, knees still bent. Without any greeting, Zeus began. "My brothers and sisters, I need to see about them. Are they like I was, chained with boxes attached to their necks?"

He'd recited their names over and over in his mind. Hestia, Hera, Hades, Poseidon, Demeter. Though he had not met them, he never wanted to forsake them the way he had been by everyone he'd known.

"They are all well, released back to Rhea as you slept. They were in a timeless state, and although older than you, all still infants. You need not worry about them right now."

"Take me back to Tartarus."

"Yet all along you wanted to come back here." Eros tilted his head.

"At first." Zeus caught his lower lip against his teeth and pressed to feel the pinch.

"I am sorry that I could not tell you the entire plan, that I gave you special ambrosia in small increments until you were immune to the Morpheous poison, then spiked your blood—"

"I don't want to hear it!"

"It was a risk we needed to take—"

"Stop talking," Zeus said, firm but not yet yelling. A heat rose in his chest and back, churning into his arms. It was the first he'd felt his power unchecked in a long while.

Eros still wore the green robe he had on in Tartarus, and it swept the floor like melted metal flowing about his feet. He knelt on the cool floor before Zeus and simply watched him, his brilliant eyes lit with intent. It would be so easy to fall into them, to become lost again, distracted.

Zeus wanted more.

"I need to get back to my father. I want to lock the chains in place myself. I want to release Chires."

"Your uncle. Hecatonchires."

"Yes."

"He is quite the beast, your uncle."

Zeus let out a fast breath. "He was good to me. He's a being who deserves to see sunlight at the very least!"

"Yes." Eros nodded, and his locks caressed his neck and shoulders. "There are many who do. Many who, like you, have lived almost all their lives as captives because they are different or misunderstood. Yet, there are others who cannot be released for they embody destruction at every level; there is, as yet, no help for them."

It was odd to be talking to Eros now. Zeus still wanted him. Still felt breathless to look upon him. But after all Zeus's suffering, his rage, Eros was cool and calm. He heard his tone as patronizing, manipulative.

"Help me accomplish this. It's the only reason I let you bring me back here. So you can help me. You owe it to me," Zeus said. "And then I never want to see you again." It was the darkness within him talking, the part of himself that had been broken by it, taken over. He could not shut it out and it made him angrier.

Anteros, standing by a sculpture of a glorious, white Pegasus, said, "Zeus, you can't!"

Eros moved away from Zeus with a rustle of soft cloth. "Anteros." The one word silenced the man who had spoken to and befriended Zeus before any of the others.

"I thought I told you to leave," Eros said.

Anteros shrugged. "I did. But I came back. I care about Zeus, too!"

Zeus watched Eros come around the chair and alongside Anteros, putting a hand against his naked, lower back. Quietly,

"All my arrows wound to the heart. He has every right to speak as he wishes, and we will help him."

Anteros turned away, shaking his head. "But why did we have to trick him? I regret it now. I want him to know that. I don't want him to leave."

Eros leaned forward and kissed Anteros on the forehead. "I know."

Zeus frowned. Eros had not said, "Neither do I." A simple: "I know." That was it.

Zeus fumed as he fought back the heat behind his eyes. He stood quickly.

"You will all help me," Zeus said hotly. "Or I will have all of you chained in Tartarus as well, since his reach is long and he answers to me now."

Eros turned his emerald stare on him, a half-smile his only softness now. Anteros's eyebrows rose and he looked shocked. Sudden tears dotted his cheeks. He turned to Eros's chest and wound his arms around his shoulders. Eros held his amoretti as he continued to watch Zeus.

Zeus snarled and strode from the room.

Chapter Thirteen

He was hurting and had been since he was born. He needed to get used to the fact that no one really cared. He'd had eighteen years to understand the idea. But after the Erotes had come and taken him to Eros's home, Zeus had seen a different way, a different world, and opened to its affection.

He saw the sham, now. It was going to be like this every time, he realized. Open yourself, and then watch people take advantage of you. Even if it was for a higher cause, he did not like it.

Zeus sat on his bed and thought about all he had learned: the idea of falling in love, sexual attraction, friendship. These concepts spurred a flame inside that felt so very different from the fires of violence his rage produced. That kind of flame felt warm and comforting; it filled the mind and body with a buoyancy that wove into the realms of pleasure, pure happiness, ecstasy. These seemed to be states of being to strive toward, not destruction, betrayal, harm.

Eros was not responsible for Cronus's behavior in wanting to hunt for and abduct his own son. But he was responsible for how he had dealt with the matter. Zeus's mind thought of a thousand different ways Eros could have handled this, and none of them involved using Zeus as bait.

Why this plan? Why now? Why give him the idea and incentive that on his own he could ever have beaten Cronus?

Of course, he could not have. Alone, he was a failure as a god and a man.

It was the worst feeling of being used, and Zeus had been so naïve. So vulnerable. He did not ever want to feel that way again. And he was not about to forgive Eros.

I wanted you, Eros, Zeus thought. *I still want you.* The unbearable pain of it made him start shaking. A heat suffused him again at the mere thought of Eros, more perfect in essence than his thunderbolt power. Desire.

He glanced about the big room, and wondered how he could still feel trapped though no chains held him now. It was as if his body was being pulled in directions he'd never had a say in. Eros. Cronus. Tartarus.

The heat of arousal interfered with Zeus's rage, and rage was what he wanted right now. He was not ready to feel it subside.

He focused on Tartarus.

Tartarus was fascinating. Zeus could feel the entity in his mind, not unlike Chires, when his uncle communicated mentally. Alien, shadowy. Tartarus was like a piece of the very edge of the darkness that had broken Zeus's mind in the end. A man cut from the starry sea.

Like Chires, Tartarus was so different it was difficult to comprehend that it lived. It seemed to breathe. It allowed people in and out of its sphere of alleys and avenues and endless halls. Cronus had taken over Tartarus's will long ago, somehow binding it to him. Zeus was not sure how.

But Tartarus had appeared to him, now, let him in. Zeus was his, or vice versa, now that Cronus was immobile. But how long would that last? Eros had said weeks. Zeus needed to make sure the chains of Tartarus held Cronus tight before those weeks were up.

He was eighteen, and all this lay heaped upon his shoulders now. He allowed himself, in this moment, to miss his naiveté, wishing he could go backward in time to the fresher moments of longing for Eros, or spying upon Hedy and Pothos making love. Or swimming with all the Erotes. He had even loved innocently spending time in the library, researching all day, sleeping there.

Zeus put a fist to his forehead, pressing down. He had to leave here or he would go crazy. He wanted to love Eros and the Erotes. But it was too much now. Distraction and frustration.

He needed more sleep. More ambrosia.

Then, he would be ready to take charge.

Chapter Fourteen

As if from a distant room, Eros's voice washed over him. "Zeus."

Zeus's skin warmed. Trickles of pleasure danced along his muscles, shivered deeper into conduits that led to veins and heart and bone. Arousal stirred him. His legs stretched out. His toes curled. The chiton he wore became too tight. He wanted it off.

A languor different from sleepiness overcame him. He wanted hands on him, lips and slick limbs. He wanted to watch Anteros swim, and Hedy and Pothos fuck again. He wanted—oh, how he wanted—Eros.

"Zeus." Now the voice was closer. As if Eros stood over the bed.

Zeus opened his eyes. He blinked against the heaviness of his newly wakened state. Eros, emerald-eyed, still in his green robe, shuffled his wings on the still air.

A pain zinged through Zeus's chest. Heat welled in his eyes and he turned away.

"What are you doing here?"

"You've slept for a very long time. I know it's going to take you a while to recover after being captive for so long. But I am worried about you."

How long had he slept? "I don't want your worry. All I want from you is to take me back to Tartarus. I know you can do it. Right now. Without a portal."

"I know."

Zeus turned back to face him, cheek tight against a silken pillow, and his body thrummed with desire to look upon him. "Yes, you know everything, all manner of secrets, don't you?"

Eros frowned, but it wasn't from anger. His mouth curved down. "You should not hate me so."

"Why?"

"I am not hated, that's why."

"Because you are the god of love? Love betrayed is part of love. It begets hatred, doesn't it?"

A long breath exhaled Eros's full, pink lips, honeying the air. "I did not betray you, Zeus. I helped you in a manner that guaranteed the best possible outcome."

"Yes, a plan that could have gone a thousand different ways." Zeus hated that he was aroused. Just the presence of Eros had him in a fevered state.

"It did not. It could not."

"Why? Because of what your precious oracle told you?" Zeus wondered what the oracle had said about Eros himself and his role in this ordeal.

"In part. There is much you do not understand."

"Because you tell me so little."

The flame-white wings drooped, creating a stab of guilt in Zeus. His mind raged in a dark fervor. But his body flamed in desire. The two battled, body and mind, and it was as if a sword sliced him right down the middle.

"I will answer all your questions."

"I don't care about answers anymore. I want to go back to Tartarus."

"You do not need to rush now and do everything at once."

Zeus sat up on the shining fuchsia bed, his palms flat at his hips, holding himself in balance. He started to swing his bare legs over the edge, but Eros moved forward so that he blocked him. Zeus wanted to kick, but also did not want the physical contact or he knew he'd be lost.

A groan of frustration surprised Zeus, because it came from his own throat. "Don't you understand? I don't want to be here."

"Anteros will be disappointed," Eros began gently.

"It's *you* I don't want to be with."

"Indeed." The tone came out low, but not sad. Or not sad enough.

Zeus slapped the bedcovers. Eros was toying with him. Pretending his words were a game. But Zeus was not playing a game. All the lavish surroundings, the pools and fountains, forest gardens and latticed rooftops, the beds and the beautiful boys would be so easy to fall into. Believe in. But who was left to trust? Even Anteros had to know Eros's secrets. And he had let on about none of them.

"Stop patronizing me." Zeus could not look at him now, the eyes so green, the face more beautiful than any imagination could conjure.

"I'm not trying to. You are Lord of Tartarus now. And this is only just the beginning for you. For nothing will ever be enough. Not for you, Zeus. Those are true words, not patronizing words."

"I cannot tell you how I—" He stopped. He wanted to say *suffered* but the word sounded so pathetic now. He was angry, not hurt. There was a difference. A huge difference.

"But I do know how you were feeling. I could feel it as well."

Zeus looked at his lap; the cotton bunched there, his arousal still aflame. Eros was reading his mind now? He blinked away sudden tears that, fortunately, did not fall.

"I don't see how you could. You were far away."

"I told you, I have an affiliation with you, Zeus, a connection. I have since you were born."

Now he looked up, the fringe of his dark lashes damp. "Why?"

"That's what I'm trying to explain to you. It happens. I was aware of your birth, aware of your dormant power. I could feel it burning in my heart. I went to the oracle and she told me your name and where you were, but that you must stay hidden until adulthood. I waited for you after you were taken to safety. I could not interfere."

"You've never told me. What exactly is this damned oracle?" For a moment, his rage rested as curiosity took over.

"She's a seer. She sees future possibilities and assesses outcomes based on the least harm. When I am confused, I seek her advice. Most gods do."

Zeus bent his legs until he could sit all the way up, wrapping his arms about his knees. He stared straight ahead, but out his peripheral vision he could see Eros, green and gold, scintillating and calm. What must it be like to have that sort of gift, to see all possibility and try to unravel it all? The chaos of it must be overwhelming. He wondered what kind of god the oracle was, if she lived in a state of constant madness.

"I can introduce you to her some day." Eros reading his mind again?

Zeus nodded slightly.

"You can hate me all you wish," Eros said. "But I am still here for you, no matter what. I will answer all your questions. I will take you wherever you wish to go. I may infect people to love one another, but I do not give my own love lightly. I do all this for you out of love. I have no other reason."

Love. Zeus rejected the notion immediately. He did not think love meant keeping secrets, or allowing the one you love to be hurt. If only Eros had told him all of this before he'd gone to Tartarus.

"Zeus, please listen. It made no difference to my existence that Cronus ruled Tartarus. Though he controlled the abyss, he was not cruel to it—to him. Everything that was done since you arrived has been to keep you from harm. Cronus was your enemy so I could not let him win. I had to send you to Tartarus. That had to be part of the plan. You had to endure a short-term of suffering to save you in the long run."

But Zeus was not ready to hear it. His body was, though. How his body wanted. Eros's nearness, his presence, washed over Zeus like a warm river. It was as if he was starving and Eros was sustenance.

Eros moved closer to the side of the bed, his knees touching it. Zeus flinched.

"I'm sorry you were hurt." A whisper on the air. The words so soothing.

"I am, too," Zeus said softly.

"I never want to see you harmed. I want to see you become more whole, grow into the person you are meant to be. You must believe me."

Zeus did believe him in that moment. But inside where the darkness leaked into him was hollowness, and a safety there that promised less pain and an indulgence in his rage. That felt good. That darkness would not be coddled. It could not see the benefit. The darkness was not in itself bad, just aloof, not unkind, but unable to give over its full self into caring about final outcomes for others. It wanted what it wanted, when it wanted.

And then there was Eros's love, shining like a mirror, sun-warmed and light-tossed, and the darkness swooned but only for the idea of Eros, the satisfaction, the possession of him.

Zeus finally turned his face up and looked at Eros, holding his gaze.

Eros's golden eyebrows rose. "It got hold of you a bit, didn't it?"

"What?"

"Your own abyss."

Zeus nodded.

The god of love took a shaky breath. "I can see it in your eyes. It's also a piece of Tartarus himself."

Zeus frowned a question.

"While he played Cronus's pet, I did not contact him. I could not. There was no entry. I did not lie to you about that. But in the beginning, eons ago, we spent much time together. I know him."

"You know this feeling, then?"

Eros offered a weak smile. "I told you I did. And your own feelings. We are affiliated, Zeus. You and I. Tartarus and

I." He let out a long breath. "It is that way even if you hate me now."

Hate. Love. Growing up. Dirty tricks. The first two were such organic, even primal, reactions. Both empowering and frightening. The second two were about life, free will. Both cruelty and kindness existed and would never go away.

Zeus felt a hand on his shoulder. Gentle. A low heat. But not the full weight.

Eros said, leaning even closer, "Please. Let me in."

He wanted so badly to lay his head on Eros's smooth, silken chest. To lose himself in him. Be cherished. Held.

He turned away.

Eros said, "You need more sleep, and then I will take you to him," and coaxed him back into the pillows.

The black sea lapped and Zeus let himself roll with it.

Chapter Fifteen

Tartarus. Like an open window letting in a cold breeze. Dark wings flapping on the edge of vision. Sound of rolling silence. Scent of lamp-oil and ice.

Zeus dreamed the table was set for four. Eros. Anteros. Himself. Tari. They were going to eat ambrosia cake topped with little god babies. But then Eros stood and made a wing-shaped light. In his arms he embraced them all, including the babies, and Tari began to cry ink tears.

Zeus woke, the dream leaving him feeling strange, still maudlin, his body still betraying him in an aroused fever. He took off his chiton and dressed himself in a leather kilt left for him on a chair by one of the Erotes. He strapped on knee-high sandals and a leather belt that wrapped once over his shoulder and once about his waist. On it he could carry anything. For now, though, he owned nothing.

The house was silent. He walked through the white halls, listening, looking.

In the pool room, along the fountains, water ran into water, chuckling. But no one was about.

He went to the library, where he found Anteros reclining naked on a red couch. He was not reading, but watching moving pictures through a hand-held window. When he saw Zeus, he sat up, putting the window aside.

"You look much better today," Anteros said.

At the sound of Anteros's voice, the dark in his mind retreated. Zeus had not realized he'd looked any different, but he supposed after his captivity and collapse, he'd returned to the house more than a little disheveled.

"Thank you."

"Are you very angry?"

How much did Anteros know? Zeus decided, because of the Erotes's connection to Eros, that he must know everything. So he nodded. "Yes."

"I'm sorry. You know I don't want you to leave."

Zeus did not want to speak of apologies. He glanced about the ornate room where shelves were lined with scrolls and books. Tapestries of abstract designs in purples and greens lined one wall.

"Where is Eros?"

Instead of answering, Anteros rose and came to Zeus. Suddenly, his arms went around Zeus's shoulders and he hugged him tight. "I knew about the special ambrosia and I said nothing. I am sorry, really. I need you to you believe that."

Zeus put his hand on the smooth arm of the golden god, feeling the slight wind of his moth-like wings as they softly shifted, and said, "You follow Eros. The plan was his doing, not yours."

Anteros stepped away, wings tight to his back. "He did everything for you. Including taint your blood. Did he tell you he gave you something to make you immune to the long sleep?"

He nodded. "All I know is that all my lessons from him were fake."

Anteros's eyes welled up with tears. "No. They were real. You needed to know, to learn about everything, strategy, discipline, all of it, and he is a great teacher. He knows."

"Yes, but none of it was practical."

Tears spilled onto a golden cheek. "You were so innocent when we brought you here. It was only weeks ago. Is that boy gone?"

"How long was I captive in Tartarus? No one has told me yet."

"Days only. Fifteen, I think."

Zeus shrugged and turned away. It had seemed so much longer. He did not want to see tears, or feel manipulated by them. The pain was still too fresh, the chains against his skin, the black box sucking his blood through an opening in his neck. And Cronus—his father—laughing at his helplessness, his naked vulnerability.

He still remembered what it felt like to be stabbed over and over in his belly, his chest. His body had healed. There weren't even scars now, though he ran his hand over the skin now and again to make sure. But his mind still reeled.

"Can you ever love us again?" Anteros asked in a low voice.

Instead of answering, Zeus asked, "Where is Eros?"

"He is at the Bridge of Stars."

"Can you take me there?"

Anteros tilted his head and let his wings unfold and stretch, fawn-gold with black spots, soft as spring petals. "Will you love me again?"

Zeus frowned, a shimmer of fire running through him at his frustration.

Anteros raised his eyebrows and pursed his lips. "The price is a kiss."

Zeus raised his arm. "Now that I have my powers back, my payment to you is I will not aim them in your direction."

Anteros pouted. "You must make that promise to me, then, forever. That I will always know your favor."

His breath caught. "Of course." He was not trying to be cruel, and Anteros had always been kind.

"Done. But I am disappointed in not receiving a kiss." He held his hand out to Zeus's threatening out-stretched arm. Zeus had not realized he'd made a fist. He uncurled his fingers and grasped Anteros, palm to palm.

As they walked out of the library and down the hall, Zeus said, "Eros knows I'm coming?"

"Yes."

"What is the Bridge of Stars?"

"It is a dream made manifest."

"I have no idea what that means."

Anteros smiled, white teeth flashing as if he gnawed all day on light. And then Zeus actually did want to kiss him. He remembered the one time they had kissed it had been the sweetest of touches. But the moment, and the request, had passed.

At the front door, which opened as if it sensed their approach, Anteros stepped onto the porch, a structure of high white columns, the deck decorated with hundreds of potted plants and trees. It was light out and the sky undulated in a pale blue wave.

Zeus had been outside the house once before. He'd noted a landscape when he'd first been flown here by the Erotes. The spongy ground of this not-Earth land grew sprigs of purple, and blue-green forests of spiky trees. No other homes were within sight, and Zeus realized this realm was Eros's realm, and no one else's.

"Where are you taking me?" Zeus asked the naked god.

Anteros's wings dragged behind him, long enough to touch the ground when he didn't bother holding them aloft. "A portal."

Zeus's stomach flipped. The last time he'd used a portal was when he'd gone to Tartarus.

"Why don't you call upon Eros to meet us here?" Zeus asked.

"He goes to the Bridge when he is troubled. I would not ask him to leave there. It's best we—you, I mean—go to him." As if sensing Zeus's worry, Anteros added, "He will accompany you to Tartarus."

The portal Anteros took Zeus to was not the one made of leaning, marble pillars. It was located on the far side of the great mansion on a purple lawn by a great Earth oak not unlike the one he'd hung from for most of his life.

Anteros knelt gracefully by a green reflecting ball.

"This is it," he said.

As Anteros bent to the alien grass, Zeus wanted to part those drooping wings that hid Anteros's buttocks and run his

144

hands down the sweet god's backside. His desire continued to shock him.

Anteros looked up, hands raised. "Come."

Zeus knelt by his side and took both hands within the clasp of his own, feeling the warmth of him, an electrical surge. Could desire kill? The one his body truly wanted was Eros, but even away from Eros it seemed his feelings could not be kept in check. It would take very little persuasion to make him want to take Anteros right here on the purple grass, fast and hard.

Their hands joined, they surrounded the reflecting ball with their arms. Anteros brought their forearms in contact with its icy surface and Zeus saw the world about them spin.

Anteros said, "Bridge of Stars."

There was a scent of burning leaves, a loud pop, and Zeus felt as if his body had been immersed in liquid, salty waves. Something to his right crashed, a sound like large pieces of wood hitting each other and glass breaking. A cacophony of singing birds followed, notes like falling stars. Zeus had heard plenty of falling stars living outside on Earth for eighteen years. They popped when they came close—the bigger ones—and sometimes gave off an anguished bird-cry.

This journey through the portal was different from the one he'd taken to Tartarus. Maybe because Anteros held his hands. Or maybe because he was going into a different sort of darkness.

One moment he was whirling through strangeness, though he felt solid ground at his feet, and the next he stood, slightly crouched, still holding Anteros's hands, in a glass dome that looked as if it floated on the very edge of space itself.

Green-robed, Eros stood on a wooden deck suspended over a whirlpool of stars. The deck had a simple, wood rail and his hands rested on it palm-down. He wings swept in great curves along his sides, white as foam. He turned his head, peeking over the edge of his left wing, as he heard them arrive.

"What happened," he said toneless, "to my request—no, my order—not to be disturbed?" He ignored Zeus, gazing directly at Anteros.

"Oh! Well…"Anteros hopped on one foot, reaching down to scratch his calf. Surrounded by dark and stars, both gods were resplendent. To gaze upon them almost hurt.

Zeus said, "I made him bring me here."

He allowed himself to look up and in the great star field arched over Eros's head he saw the bridge. A billion stars looked twisted or braided to form an arc, a river of golds and lavenders and pinks, upon the dark edge of space. No, not a river, a span over it, for the river was the black of space that swept in all about the gathered glints of light. It looked as if some god had thrown all the faceted gemstones in existence up to the skies and they froze there in mid-motion.

Zeus could not hide his gasp. He moved away from the reflecting ball that sat on the otherwise empty deck.

Eros turned his gaze onto him. "You look better rested now."

"I am." His heart churned in his chest. Eros looked like liquid light and even the very darkness in Zeus swooned to see him.

Forlorn though he still felt, he needed this being to guide him, encompass him.

"I am ready to back to the abyss."

"It is a lot of responsibility for a very young god," Eros said.

"I will learn."

Eros nodded, eyes downcast now. "Very well. I will take you to him."

Zeus's chest quaked. He felt as if Eros had touched him, but nothing outward moved between them.

"Anteros, would you like to come along?"

"To the abyss? No thank you!" He tossed his golden hair with a shake of his head, placed both palms on the reflecting ball, and said to the air, "Nest of Eros," and vanished.

"You will have to take my hand," Eros said, lifting his arm.

Zeus curved his palm into Eros's hand and the journey began. Different from the other two portal journeys he'd remembered, smooth and white, like being wrapped in ivory clouds, and with only the sound of the humming wind, low and pleasant and filled with summer secrets.

Chapter Sixteen

They landed in a dimly lit hall. The clouds cleared, and Zeus recognized the breathing corridors, the many endless, nameless doors, and echoes like hushed breathing all around.

Eros led Zeus forward and around a bend, where the flooring sloped to curving, metal stairs that led down into shadow. The metal dripped with condensation, as if it had just rained.

"The pits?" Zeus asked, self-consciously pulling his hand away.

Eros nodded. "Tartarus took everyone at the party down into there to hold them, everyone who was willingly going to drink your blood. Including your father. That is where you wanted to go, is it not?"

Swallowing hard, Zeus nodded.

Eros led the way in a dazzling radiance that seemed so out of place. Around and around they went, deeper into the abyss, their sandaled feet tapping against the damp iron steps. It might have taken minutes, or hours. Zeus could not be sure of anything, including time down here. Cold air wafted over them, bringing ghosts of fog that intermittently obscured his vision.

In the pits, the fog of Tartarus smelled of winter, cold and grieving, but also strangely sweet.

When the stairs finally ended, they entered a great dungeon room, long and endless, stretching as far as Zeus could see. He expected the people held there to be chained or worse, much as he had been, but instead saw rows and rows of glass chambers on their sides, stacked six high. Within lay beings. Hundreds of them. They looked to be fast asleep.

"These people are alive?" Zeus asked.

"Of course. Under Cronus's rule, many were given dreams to entertain them, not all good dreams. But his rule is ended. Tartarus has no reason to torture those he holds. But the final decision is yours now."

"It's so silent down here. So death-like."

As Zeus spoke, an image of a man moved slowly from the shadows, as if floating. He looked to be about Zeus's height, but he had no features that Zeus could see. He was a silhouette in a man's form, cut from dark itself. As he approached, he spoke, his voice a low echo.

"Eros. Zeus. Welcome."

The figure wavered and a man's face appeared, dark-haired, undulating. His arms rose as he approached. Eros and the two embraced tight.

"It's been a long time, Eros."

"Tari," said Eros, smiling, and holding the being's ever-changing face between his hands, kissing him on the mouth.

Zeus stirred to see this, but realized they were both older than the universe itself. They had known each other for a longer time than he could even imagine.

Eros let Tari go and they both turned to Zeus.

"Here is your new king," Eros said.

"Ah, Zeus, the beautiful god of the thunder. Welcome. I am yours to command now."

Zeus did not know what to think or say. He had felt this edge of darkness, this cloak of the abyss entering into him building upon a hollowness and resentment he'd been denying for his entire life. He had thought the abyss to be comprised of these things, but meeting Tari, he saw only that Tari reflected, in his dark mirror, the best and worst of those he touched. He was the perfect prison warden, for every punishment within his scope of influence on the mind fit its prisoner's guilt, and every good deed might be rewarded with answering pleasure.

"You seem to have it well in hand," Zeus finally said, feeling suddenly younger than his years, a child still learning to navigate.

"I do. But I welcome your strength, young god."

Tari stepped toward Zeus and embraced him. It was like being embraced by wind, though now the man's features had stabilized more into a smooth-cheeked youth with dark hair spiking about his face. The rest of his body appeared unclothed, but hidden in shadow. Or perhaps he wore the dark as a cloak, the way Zeus envisioned it within himself.

"Where is my father?" Zeus asked.

Tari bowed. "I will take you to him."

Down rows of glass chambers, they walked. The silence became a loud hum. Only their footfalls proved life still existed in this dungeon of endless sleep.

After passing dozens of stacked bodies, their arms folded in repose, their faces obscured by fog, Tari stopped.

"Here," he said. He pointed to the top-most chamber of one stack. When he moved his hand, the chamber floated up and to the side, then gently landed before them at their feet.

Zeus peered into the glass top and saw the black hair, the fine features, and the lithe but very tall body in a wrinkled, knee-length white chiton. The sandals were gone. His father looked innocent and young, not a monster at all.

Behind the glass, the Titan body trembled, and the arms began to move. Eyelids flicked back. Dark eyes lit to waking, and a quick madness flamed them. Cronus opened his mouth and yelled in a wordless howl. Then he began to kick and pound the glass faster and faster, as if a panic seized him and he could not stop.

Zeus made out muffled words as Cronus began to speak. "Let me out! Let me out!"

Tari stood, dark and shining, arms crossed, and said, "What would you like done with him, my king?"

"Can he be calmed so I may speak with him?"

A fog filled the glass coffin and Cronus's body went limp. But the eyes remained open, staring, mad.

"Can he hear us?" Zeus asked.

"Yes. Loud and clear."

"Cronus, I sentence you to the pit for ten thousand years. More if I deem it necessary."

Cronus's mouth turned down. He spat at the glass. "Do you think I care about your sentencing? About the pit? After all this time? Kings come and go, Zeus. You will have your time and then your fate, too, will be the pit. It happens to us all."

Zeus flinched before he could catch himself, and glanced to Eros for help. Eros gave him a kind nod. One Zeus did not think he deserved, but welcomed anyway.

Despite the reassurance, a flame lit deep inside him.

"Eros, I see you have deigned to sully your feet in the pit you claimed you'd never again set foot in. Why has no one ripped your wings off yet?" Cronus hissed.

Zeus was horrified at Cronus's anger, but not surprised. This was a man who'd tried to harm him. A god who ate his own spawn. And yet, as his father, he had the power to make Zeus feel small, underrated, unworthy. He had been the cause of all Zeus's abnormal childhood, his suffering, his incarceration.

What Zeus really wanted to do to Cronus was tear him into pieces and leave those pieces writhing for all of eternity. What kind of boy had he become that he could even think this?

Tari touched Zeus lightly on the arm, a cool leaf-caress. The echo-voice said, "The wounded do heal."

Cronus frowned when he saw their rapport.

"Why have you even wakened me? What do you want from me?" Cronus asked.

"Only to see you one last time, Father." Zeus tensed, trying to tamp down on his outrage.

Cronus tossed his head back and forth, unable to do more than that under the drug of the fog, and in such a small chamber. "I am not your father. Remember that! You are what formed from the spit of my body, that's all. I never had a thought to making you, though you have turned out quite splendidly, haven't you?"

Zeus gritted his teeth. Once again the lightning tried to push through him. He held his breath against the flow. How could someone whom he had never met hate him so much?

"I know that now, Cronus." His mouth trembled to say the name. But he would never call him *Father* again. "There was never to be a father's love for me, no matter what. I see that now."

"Is that what you wanted? What you thought you deserved?"

The question stunned him. Everything he'd endured to this point in his life had been his father's fault. "No, but I did not deserve such hate."

"Hate, you say. You're a fool. And you'll rule as a fool. I regret the night I planted you inside your mother."

As if physically slapped, Zeus stepped back. Without thinking, he raised his hand and the lightning shot forth. He had not had time to feel it build so high. It hit the side of the glass with a loud crash, lighting all the glass boxes in the room orange.

Safe inside, Cronus began to laugh and laugh.

Eros and Tari backed away. Eros yelled, "Zeus!"

Zeus's lightning kept surging, his fingertips itching, stinging, and he let out a roaring cry as he felt his body begin to weaken and the flame flicker to a thin green thread, then short out.

Zeus snarled. "I want him hurting! I want him dead!"

Eros came immediately to his side, touching his back. "He can't die."

Cronus, unharmed, craned his head toward Eros.

"Let Eros be your father, brother, lover. He is well-trained in simpering platitudes of the weaker organ called the heart. Mine I left behind long ago, cast to an Earth sea and turned to ocean weed and muck along with my father's rotted balls, and I have never once looked back. I tell you, I am more content for it. If I can give you some advice, Zeus, when you rule with the heart, expect much pain."

Zeus smacked the glass with his fists. "Shut up!" His chest quivered with distress. "You don't get to say anything anymore!"

Cronus continued to laugh.

Zeus shut his eyes and turned stiffly away.

Pain. Cronus had talked about it as if he did not inflict it, but encompassed it. What had ever hurt Cronus? Zeus had read as many stories about his life and his deeds as he could stomach. A long existence of affairs and wars, but also a long life of peace and euphoria.

When had Cronus gone mad?

After awhile, he turned back. Cronus lay in a stupor, all laughter gone, but still stretching his limbs, twitching as his rage pushed through him forcing him to fight against his imprisonment. Zeus knew that rage. Lately, it never left him. Was he destined to become just like his father so soon?

He stepped further away, his back to the coffin, hating himself in this moment, glancing helplessly toward Eros. Only eighteen, and still very much a boy, the weight of everything was too much.

Eros turned to meet his gaze.

Zeus wanted out of the pits now. He clasped his hands behind his back to keep them from shaking. Why had he wanted to come back here? To see Cronus? He'd been stupid to leave Eros's house this second time, when it had not been forced onto him. The comforts. The warmth. The love of the Erotes. All that should have been enough.

But he also knew he would never be able to rest until he had seen Cronus one last time.

Zeus watched Eros's sleek brows lower. His lips parted a fraction. One wing stretched toward him, not touching, but shading his right side. Zeus let out a held breath. Eros inhaled deeply, as if he were breathing for Zeus, and gave him a slight nod.

This was Zeus's responsibility now. Tartarus. Tari. All its inhabitants, its prisoners. It was all his. He shivered. He didn't want it.

Then he thought of Chires. He had the power now to free him.

Zeus turned to Tari. He motioned toward his father's glass coffin. "Put him back. Out of my sight forever. Away from my thoughts." His words came out shaky.

Tari nodded, motioning with his hand, and the chamber rose with Cronus, still restless, within.

"I have one other request before I leave," Zeus said. His voice sounded strange in his ears, hollow and faraway. "Can you free Chires?"

"Hecatonchires?"

"Yes. My uncle."

"He may not be suited to be on his own," Tari replied, turning away.

"Who is?" Eros asked.

Zeus glanced at him. Eros smiled.

"I want him freed," Zeus said, clearing his throat, half-whispering.

"Where would he go?"

"Anywhere he wishes. He can stay and assist here if he wants. But I will no longer tolerate him being chained."

"You don't know him," Tari warned. "Just because you shared a cell with him for a short time, doesn't mean you understand him."

"I know enough. I felt him in my mind, heard him. He was good and I want him freed!" He'd gotten his wind back.

"Then," Tari said, bowing, "it is done, my king."

"I'm ready to leave now," Zeus said to Eros. His entire body felt hot and cold at the same time. Sweaty. Weak. Pained.

Tari said, "I was hoping you would stay, my king. For your realm starts here and will expand, but you need to know this place better first. As a beginning point."

He did not feel like a king. Not now. Not after seeing his father's madness, hearing that his own father thought him not worthy to be born.

Eros stepped closer to Zeus, and said, "He needs more time. He will come with me for awhile."

He realized it was all madness. Even Eros in his life. From the moment of his birth and he was hung from a tree in a hemp harness, then taken by men with wings to meet his fate— he was guaranteed an existence filled with insanity.

He thought back on those boys who had once entered his green spring glade, carefree, at play, teasing him because they knew no better, and wondered about an ordinary life like that, wondered about all he had missed.

He clasped his hands into fists at his side. His lightning gift had returned, but what use was it except for destruction? He'd killed four boys with it when he was twelve. He'd also raised them from the dead. But were those boys ever the same innocent children after that? Had his mark on them stained them for life? He could not know. What good was his heat, his energy if all it could do was explode forth from his body in anger, and scare and hurt and kill people?

The cloak of darkness in his own mind threatened to wrap him entirely.

"He needs rest," Eros said.

"You will make sure he is taken care of then?" Tari asked. He seemed genuinely concerned.

Eros, blinding and ever-infuriating, said, "I will."

They were talking about him as if he were a baby, unable to fend for himself. Maybe it was true.

Zeus wanted those golden arms around him. Wanted to feel the safety of that large house again. The library. And all rivers and forests the arboretum held within. And outside, the porch, the purple grass, the trees, and that faraway deck under a bubble of glass overlooking the Bridge of Stars that Anteros said Eros favored.

He blinked as Eros took his hand.

The shifting face of Tari turned toward Zeus's, a whirl of stars between them—much like the Bridge.

Tari said, "I will wait as I have waited for a thousand years and more."

Then Tari laughed, not like Cronus, but smooth and with pleasure, brighter than darkest dark, the dungeon echoing, moaning as if it hated to hear that sound of mirth where only shadows were allowed to play. But the dungeon *was* Tari, bleak and wintry and breathing, just as the laughter was Tari, intelligent and dazzling.

Zeus had no idea what to make of it as Eros's hand tightened, and Eros said, "Come. Now."

Before that last word *"now"* had settled into Zeus's mind, his senses tangled and got mixed up: he smelled a green light, felt a loud clang, and heard a feather touch his cheek. Everything became confused, and then he was standing in the pool room and beautiful naked men with wings swam in a sapphire, liquid square surrounded by happy, frothing marble fountains of dolphins and mermen.

Zeus let out a breath like a sob. It felt as if he'd been holding it for the entire time in the pits of Tartarus.

Chapter Seventeen

Eros said, "Sit."

A leather couch draped in purple, a cushioned back: It caught him as he fell more than sat, his knees giving way.

Zeus focused on little things to get his bearings. The way the edges of Eros's wings furred in white delicacy, softer than lace. How the water behind him quivered as if about to break, but always staying in one piece, as liquid tended to do unless frozen.

The heat of Eros was like a hearth, or maybe a star. Perhaps he'd been born a star if he was a primordial, and he wanted to laugh at that thought but nothing came out.

Eros said, "Close your eyes."

Zeus turned away, staring at where warm, sun-colored tile met a smooth, white wall.

"Zeus, please do this one thing for me."

Zeus turned his head, his gaze meeting the emerald depths of Eros's eyes. Irresistible. This god. Of love.

His eyelids drooped. He shut them tighter and did not see darkness but all color mirroring the shapes of the pool room, then warping into new designs until it all quieted to a mute gray landscape.

During those seconds, he felt a hand at his brow, fingers coming along the left side of his forehead. He felt the couch dip and knew Eros came to sit beside him.

He sat very still, back against the soft cloth, head slightly forward, but could not completely relax. His fingers curled so that his nails bit into his palms. His thighs were clenched, the skin of his arms and chest tight.

"If you are too long in the abyss it warps your mind. But in the end, we all head toward, and come from, the dark. Windswept. Shattering. Landing. Nesting. Our wings unfurled. Our hearts still and forever on fire."

First the voice of Eros went into him like notes of a strange song he'd never heard. Then the meaning of the words touched inside him, bits of light blooming like a garden of still-wet, fragile flowers piercing the cloak around him.

He kept his eyes closed and the fingers in his hair moved back and forth. The heat of the man beside him grew. He wanted to rest in that fever, and his skin heated at the thought.

"You are a man now, but you are still in so many ways just a badly hurt boy."

He did not want to hear the way the tone swept through him, touching all the barriers inside him, making them into mere dust floating in a long-abandoned room. But it was too late. The words took hold. The remnants of the icy cage from Tartarus melted, the last vestiges evaporating to stardust.

He heard a single note, then, low and far, strangely painful, and realized it came from his own throat.

It was as if he'd run a long distance and could not catch his breath. The muscles around his eyes hurt. His throat ached. He could not speak. He felt a hand against his back. Then he was falling again, and arms caught him. A softness, like a blanket, surrounded him. Feather-light. His eyes began to leak and he could not stop it.

His body shook.

He thought he felt the fires begin to rise inside him again, but they abated as he let himself ease further into the strong arms, chest shaking, water on his cheeks.

He drew his legs up, curled into the lap that supported his side, his back against Eros's chest. He became exhausted at his body's rending. The ripping and tearing, then the way the system put itself back together. Was this a god-talent, too?

Whatever it was, it brought catharsis. For a while he rested until his body felt like his again. Until he could understand that he lived, he was whole, he was held.

When he finally opened his eyes, lashes sticky, he was looking up at the ceiling showing bright stars beyond. His head rested on a firm thigh. The rest of his body was covered in a white cocoon; Eros's wings draped about them both, front to back, fluttering gently against the backs of his calves.

One of Eros's hands was still at his head, fingers threaded through his hair. The other curved about his waist.

Eros's upper body leaned back against the couch. His head tilted to the side. He was staring past Zeus's shoulders at seemingly nothing. They were both very still, but Zeus could feel the pulse of him against his back, and a warm tremble like held-back power so great not even the idea of it could contain it.

How long had Zeus forgotten that Eros and the Erotes also held inside them seething energy, a churning, vital longing that threatened to burn its container up every hour of every day? They all had it. It was what made them gods. Their god-gifts might represent as something other than thunderbolts, but they were there inside each and every one of them.

Zeus was not alone.

He turned his body slightly, feeling the press of the leather kilt he'd donned earlier that morning. It pinched the skin at his waist. Eros's arms tightened.

All the warmth from deep inside him that so often in the past weeks had turned to fire and lightning, flooded through him now like a gentle current. As if he basked in a flowing, summer river, his skin flushed head to toe. He waited for the power to increase, the gentle suffusion to turn to stabbing flame. But that did not happen. The warmth remained gentle, soothing, and pooled in the center of his stomach radiating outward.

Zeus sighed at the contentment he felt, letting his muscles go lax again. Eros shifted his upper body and placed a kiss on the hair at the back of his head.

159

He had his arms curled against his chest and let them fall
forward until one palm rested against Eros's knee, the other arm
bent against Eros's thigh. The skin was so warm beneath the
green robe. All of Eros surrounding him was warm and white
and luxurious. The wings made a soft cave of silver shade.

Feeling languid and bold at the same time, Zeus turned
until he was face up and could look into Eros's face. Golden
locks brushed across one side of his face. The eyes brewed with
spring and suppleness, essence of Zeus's childhood glade. Only
now Zeus wasn't trapped. He was grown. A man. King of
Tartarus.

Eros's arms were firm in their grasp, but not in a way
that Zeus associated with a cage. He was free now. To choose
where he wanted to be, who he wanted to be with. He wanted
those arms around him, holding him, letting him be still inside,
quiet so he could finally breathe. Finally just *be.*

The high cheekbones stretched under impossibly golden
skin. The chin curved with a perfect shallow dimple. Zeus's
gaze took him all in, the way the lashes looked darker brown
because of their thickness, the curve of the silky brows like gilt
paint. Eros's breath came over him, honey-sweet with a hint of
apple tartness.

Zeus could never deny how much he had wanted him
since the day they'd met. But something in his mind, his heart
still murmured, criticizing the betrayals, all of them he'd
experienced recently, including the body itself.

He could not keep his thoughts to himself, the will to
challenge too strong, the rage he'd felt like a scrape that had not
begun to heal.

"Is this a lie, too?"

"In your heart, you will know the answer."

"My heart is disturbed and cannot be trusted."

"Is that what you think?"

Zeus nodded. "I know."

Eros put a hand on his naked chest, over the center, his
fingers drawing tiny, slow circles. "Your heart is vast and

160

brilliant, like the core of a star. It can always be counted on to tell you what you need to know. If you think it is disturbed you are thinking too much. The heart does not think. It just feels."

"I feel betrayed. All the time. I can't stop." His vision prickled at his honest statement.

"By me? By Cronus? By your own heart?"

"All of it."

Eros brushed his lips across Zeus's brow. "The greatest of betrayals are not personal. They are always about something else, not you. What another wants. What they can achieve. Sometimes even for the greater good. You may feel they hurt you, but they are impersonal."

"You lied to me, Eros." Now Zeus put his hands between them and pushed himself up a little.

"Not to harm you. Not ever. Only to help."

Zeus closed his eyes, feeling the lashes meet. "I was harmed!"

"You would have been harmed worse if I had not." So soft, the music of his voice. Zeus wanted to believe in him, to trust.

"I cannot help but blame you for Cronus hurting me."

"I know."

"And my own heart." His throat trembled. Should he say his thoughts or not? He swallowed hard. "I am in love with you and I don't even know if that is real."

"You are asking the god of love if love is real?"

"No, I'm asking if my love is."

Eros leaned down, kissing his bangs, smiling into them. Zeus could feel his mouth open wide, the breath fluff his hair as he spoke. "Love is not a shield, Zeus. It is the taking away of shields."

Zeus grunted.

"You cannot have rules and barriers and conditions for what trust might mean to you, and then call upon love as well. All the things you do to protect your heart, to cushion the vulnerability of your own feelings, are but demons to true love.

161

Those demons eat at love. They create possessive love, jealousies, resentments, high expectations that can never be met. They are love's misery demons living in the abstract reaches of the endless seas of the mind for human and god alike. But in that mind-sea are also so many scintillating breaths of light, poison to the demons."

As Eros's speech washed over him, Zeus felt as if he were rocking in those gentle arms.

"These breaths are love's starlight and summer dreamings, love's homeworld of gilt and luster, of ardent pleasure reaching, filling, undulating. The tension of need and building pleasure of the body. The beauty of the red moment of ecstasy healing you like a sound of wind through lutes, or the scent of life at the edges of a warm lake filled with stars. The taste, my young sweet god, of spirit itself, is all fire and salt and purity made of love."

Zeus realized his mouth had gone slack. He gazed at Eros and heard the speech as if from a land of dream, understanding on levels greater than mere words.

His heart recognized these things. He was just afraid.

He trembled.

"It is original fear that trembles," Eros said.

"No. It's not," Zeus murmured. "It's desire."

Eros chuckled against his temple. Drew him closer. Zeus let him, not pushing now, but grasping at Eros's chest, fingertips edging the nipples under the green robe, riding lower to feel the ripple of ribs beneath.

Eros moved over him, his wings going up, then coming back around them both, sweeping the marble, pool-room floor. He grasped Zeus behind the head and pulled him up, kissing him on the lips, soft at first as if finding his way, then deeper, lips parting, suckling, tongue probing.

Zeus had no recourse but to kiss him back. One moment of hesitation led to the next where all he wanted was more and more.

Eros pulled back, and Zeus was bereft, staring up at him confused.

"Will you come with me to my bed?"

Eros's bed. He had never even seen it. Thought perhaps it was rumor that the god even slept.

Zeus turned his face into Eros's chest. "I don't know if I can move."

"You don't have to."

Zeus felt a small breeze, a half-twirl of reality, and sighed against a fragrance of flowers. Before he could blink he was lying against warm cushions, the smoothness of shining sheets rubbing his back and legs, and a gold god's arms still wrapped about his waist and chest.

It wasn't fair that all the non-primordials needed portals. Eros could just pop in and out of places. But it was nice that he could take people with him.

Whiteness fluttered. Eros tightened his wings against his back.

Zeus missed the tent they'd made, the private sensation of hiding, the idea of protection.

Legs stretching, Zeus felt Eros roll into him. He watched the beautiful hands move up and take his head again, watched as Eros came close until their lips met. Their bodies met. Their wills met.

He had wanted to run free his whole life. Now it felt as if that were happening. He stopped breathing and felt the kiss push its way into him, the reverberations of it rocking through his whole body.

He had lived the laws of being shackled, of pain, of cold, of the terrible and wonderful fire within. He wanted the law of love now. More than anything.

A quick thought crossed his mind and he pulled back with a jerk.

"What's wrong?"

Zeus said, "Will we forget this some day? Will we some day go into the Lethe and dream and forget?"

"Perhaps. But not for a long while. And even when it happens, we'll be made new again, and we'll find each other again."

"How can you be sure?"

"We are connected, Zeus. I am sure."

Zeus took a quick breath. Connected. He wanted to believe it.

"Relax. You learned patience at an early age. Go into that now. Be in the moment."

Nervous, Zeus forced his muscles to unknot, slacken. Talented hands helped, running up and down his sides, over his shoulders, a light massage. They lifted the leather sash off and away. They moved low again, undoing his kilt. He had to lift his hips for it to be taken all the way off.

Eros leaned away and sat up, pulling his robe off. It gave way at his wings and easily slid to the floor.

Lean and glistening. Ancient and young. Wings drawn tight so that they looked like a short, feathered cloak clinging to his back. Hair like melted sun. Eros was ardor incarnate. Elegance. Grace in all the colors of light.

Against the cream-colored sheets, Zeus's deep brown skin felt rough to him, and he was more thickly muscled, awkward. The black hair that fell into his eyes was like a reminder of the cloak of darkness that threatened him.

As he was comparing their appearances in his thoughts, Eros interrupted. "Remember what I showed you in the mirror? You are more lovely than ever," and ran his hand down the middle of Zeus's chest, over his flat belly, stopping only where the edge of his hip stretched the skin of his abdomen.

He was *lovely*. Pleasure at that word coursed through him. Zeus clutched his lower lip between his teeth and watched the god of love for his next move.

Eros raised his eyebrows. Asking for permission.

Zeus let out the breath he'd been holding and searched his body for any hint that it might lose control, explode outward, send Eros flying with a surge of flame and booming thunder. But the warmth within that grew hotter was not that of his power. It was desire, and need, and it lapped in waves and tides against his skin and in his veins.

He wanted to be touched. By Eros and no one else.

He nodded once, and only then did Eros continue to draw his hand down, lower and lower until he touched the fevered evidence of Zeus's longing. His love.

His already hard cock stiffened more, sending him reeling as Eros ran his palm over it. The fingers curved against the underside, moving to a smooth but firm embrace. He slowly squeezed, his hand gently milking.

The sensation caused his back to arch. Zeus had never felt such pleasure, not even when Anteros had tried—and pretty much succeeded—in seducing him, making his lightning come forth. That had been good but out of control, his mind unsure, and not this intense. Now Eros held him and all his longing was focused. A low moan escaped his tight lips.

He felt as if he was reaching for something beyond his perception. A grand continuation beyond reality. A sensation of rising and falling at the same time.

Eros. Essence of candles, hearts, arrows, kisses. Yet all of that was decorative flourish, the painted symbol. Not the authentic person behind the god-mask.

It seemed almost silly to feel final devotion in a merely physical act, but when Eros said, "May I kiss you here, as I did your lips?" Zeus lost all sense of time.

He could only nod as Eros lowered his head and gently put his lips to the crown of his erection. The beautiful mouth moved slowly, pressing, pulling, taking him into a hint of hot and damp, and it felt too wonderful to remain so still. Zeus pushed up, stretching his legs out, then pulling them up, and groaned, his breath coming fast.

Eros took him deeper, pulling all sensation he could from him, and Zeus cried out as his pleasure built and built. His hands fisted the coverlet and sheets. His hips rocked. Eros's

165

palms held his hips down flat and kept control, kept up the generous motions of his mouth, the ecstatic sucking.

Zeus could not see anymore. The light went away but instead of dark replacing it, more light filled his vision, white and pure like exploding suns, rivers of it foaming, streaming, a blinding dawn. His body was light. His brain. His mind. And all that was meant to be was in this moment of pleasure, of basking in the embrace of true love.

He wanted it to last. It could not. At this point, denying his own orgasm was an impossible task, even for a god. The pinnacle of his desire ripped through him and his cock jerked, pulsing in hard bursts. Breath held, the petals of himself unfolding, he came with a yell, a cry, a wrenching sob.

Salt and sweet in the back of his mouth. The scent of orchids. Honey. His breath caught over and over.

Eros drew away, still petting him, drawing out the pleasure, the sacred trust of close embraces, as if promising to never leave. For that was what his touch communicated. No need for words. Just a sweet caress of *I will never leave.*

There had been no thunder, no lightning, and no destruction. Only beauty and giving and pleasure.

Zeus rolled into his arms. The wings shushed against the air, rising, coming over them both. Zeus could not get his arms past Eros's waist. The wings were in the way. So he lifted his embrace up to Eros's shoulders and his arms came around to the center of his upper back where soft down met his fingertips.

Eros gave a small sound of approval and kissed him. Then he rose up and said, "You do not look disappointed."

"No." He wanted to say more. Wanted to shout, *It was everything.* But his voice failed him.

Eros chuckled softly against his cheek.

"Don't worry. You are young. It will happen fast like that at first. Again and again. We will do this often."

"We will?"

"If you wish."

"Oh, I wish," Zeus blurted. His breath came fast. He moved to topple Eros, and pushed him onto his back with little care to his wings. But Eros was used to his wings, and they folded quickly up and back as Zeus balanced himself with his arms on either side of the long golden body, his hips now between Eros's spread thighs. He felt the love god's cock press hot and unresisting to his stomach. Everything about them was drenched in arousal, the very air misted with their perfumes of love, their need, their want.

Eros's skin glistened. Velvet and hard muscled, softer at cheek, at thigh, at buttock. But his chest was stone, lean muscle sculpted like a marble relief. His stomach was taught and trembling. Zeus leaned on one arm and examined all of Eros with his free hand, touching everywhere he could reach, and Eros let him, head back, lashes a thin dark line against his cheeks, mouth up-curved.

Mostly hairless but for his head, eyebrows, and lashes, Eros had a dusting of tight blond curls framing his cock. Zeus finally touched that centered power and wrapped his fingers about it. The cock twitched and leaked fluid onto his hand. He did not ask permission the way Eros had, he just did as he pleased, lowering himself so he could lick that clear stream of arousal. Bitter and sweet at the same time. His tongue swirled and before he knew it he was sucking it down, the entire length, feeling it stretch his mouth.

Eros hissed. But did not protest.

Zeus's dark hair fluttered about the hips, the flat belly. His chin touched the god's taut balls, firm, round, softer perhaps than the wings. He reached with one hand between the golden thighs and cupped those balls, letting them shift over his fingers, squeezing very gently as he sucked.

Eros lifted his hips and thrust into Zeus's mouth. Liking the sensation, Zeus stilled his head and let that cock move in and out between his tight lips, his tongue working shaft and tip over and over.

He did not know—or care—how long it lasted. He just wanted to keep doing this and never stop.

He felt the spurt before he heard Eros cry out. Then his mouth was full, over-full, and he could not swallow fast enough. Spent pleasure dripped from his lips as Eros pulled his cock back and reached up, cupping Zeus's chin. He brought Zeus up in the bed and they kissed until Zeus could no longer taste the thick liquid but only Eros's sweet mouth, lips and tongue.

Zeus was hard again. Stiff as a new green stalk coming up from the Earth.

He felt the answering desire in Eros, and their explorations began anew. Sometimes frantic. Sometimes lazy, barely touching until they could not stand it anymore and came together rubbing, groaning.

Eros was the first to offer himself, spreading his long legs and lifting himself onto a pillow. He narrowed his brows. His chin jutted forward in mock nonchalance.

"Just take me," he said, reaching down beyond his spread thighs, rolling back a bit and using his fingers to spread his buttocks.

A rosy bud promised a tight entrance, a channel of thrusting pleasure. Zeus had seen Hedy and Pothos fuck like that. He'd been shocked and turned on at the same time.

"Will it hurt?" Zeus looked up.

Eros rolled his eyes. "Not for a god."

He could not stop his hand from going to that opening, touching, feeling the pucker. He leaned down and licked there to make it wet, tasting clean, hot flesh and the promise of more heat. Eros kept saying, "Oh yes, oh yes!"

But Zeus was unsure about what more to do.

Gently, Eros said, "Open me with your fingers."

It was awkward, even though Eros opened to him. Zeus felt too much resistance.

Sitting up, Eros opened a cupboard over the bed and handed Zeus a cool, small flask. "Would you like some oil?"

Instantly, he knew what to do, and he wasted no time oiling the little hole and then his fingers, and later, his cock.

Eros gave him lots of compliments, and began to talk a little dirty. He said things that made Zeus's mind reel, such as "shove harder" when he put two fingers inside him, and "I want to feel that pretty pink tip right at the edge, ready to breech me" as he pushed himself up a little and grabbed Zeus's cock, stroking, thumbing the smooth, oiled head. Swollen with pleasure, Zeus pulled back his fingers and with Eros guiding him, placed his cock against the opening.

"Push now," Eros instructed.

Zeus did but not hard enough to get all the way in. But Eros led him on, "deeper! deeper!" and the heat and tightness surrounding his cock made Zeus crazed. He got his balance and pushed harder until he felt his balls bounce against Eros's buttocks.

Eros sighed, his blond hair framing his face in golden rays all about him on the pillow. He tilted his head back, closed his eyes and said, "Just fuck me until you can't anymore."

Zeus began to move, cock gliding in and out, so sweet, so amazing the way Eros's heated body milked him. The faster he fucked, the more Eros yelled. The more Zeus yelled. Up and down his hips went, his cock getting hotter, everything around him blasting away into a million pieces, to dust, to nothing. He watched as dark flesh met and sank into pale gold, the rosy edges of the hole constricting about his shaft.

When he exploded, Eros came too, a gush of white liquid spilling over the head of his cock and onto his belly.

Later, Zeus said, "That was pleasurable to you?"

Eros grinned, white teeth flashing. "Let me show you something. Lie back."

Zeus lay back away from the wet spots they'd just made on the sheets, and Eros petted him slowly, encouraging him to spread. "Lift your legs up and back," he said.

"I'm not sure."

Eros leaned down and whispered, "It's all right, I'm not going to fuck you." His smile touched Zeus's lips. "Yet."

Zeus watched as Eros put oil on his fingers and caressed first his balls, then further back, gently sliding against his hole. Slowly, the finger penetrated. It didn't hurt, but Zeus gasped anyway.

"Did you ever wonder why we are made like this, so human-like if we don't use our holes to defecate?"

Zeus shook his head. He didn't know, or think about it. In fact, the organ was not really real to him, just there, like his bellybutton.

"Because of this," Eros said. He pushed deeper into Zeus, his finger sliding gently along the inside wall until he hit something that made Zeus jump.

"There," Eros said.

"What?" Zeus's mouth fell open as Eros stroked that place inside him again, firmer.

He sighed in pleasure. "Do that more!"

"Of course," and Eros continued until Zeus was writhing and came so fast he could not believe that he'd just fucked Eros and come minutes before.

"Is that how it felt for you when I...?"

"Yes," Eros said, and leaned down, petting his softening cock, kissing the tip, suckling at it, then moving up to kiss his lips. "You are so beautiful. It is such an honor to love you."

Zeus started to tremble at the words, his mouth shaking, his throat tightening, but Eros kissed harder and the tremble turned to immersion in caring, sharing, love.

For hours they made love. The hours turned to a day and a night. They napped and fucked, and days passed. Zeus wanted nothing more than this. Forever.

Epilog

Zeus woke and basked in the stillness for a while. Eros still slept, a vision of bronze beside him. He lifted Eros's head from where it rested against his chest, the blond locks caressing his nipple, and gently placed a pillow under his head. Then he sat up, getting his bearings.

The white and lavender room smelled of spring and faint rain rivers, fresh and clean. If he listened hard, he could almost hear the breeze. Everything was so quiet. Divine. Zeus was sated and at peace. He searched his mind for the darkness. For now it had receded. The fire within him was but an orange spark, tiny as a stone in a child's ring.

The only burning he felt was unabated desire. The man— the god—sleeping beside him held his heart. Zeus forgot all his hate, but still wondered at what might happen next. He knew almost nothing about love. Giving his heart away might be a huge mistake. But it could not be helped anymore than he could help it that he breathed, or that his spirit was made from flame.

He lay back and stared at the decorative ceiling and thought he could live like this forever if he chose. He was a god. An up and coming king. Who would deny him?

He looked down at himself, his dark body next to the pale gleam of Eros. The two of them entwined was a beautiful thing.

He saw Eros had awakened and was looking at him. That green gaze never ceased to amaze him, the color so vivid and rich. Eros smiled and Zeus warmed from the top of his head to the tips of his toes.

"We've been in here for days. I feel like a swim," he said.

171

Zeus said, "Yes." Cool water against the fever of his skin would be wonderful. And afterward, he hoped, more caresses and kisses.

Hand in hand, they walked the white hall to the pool room where azure waters waited.

Zeus jumped into them, naked and unafraid now, and the pool enfolded him, welcoming, as if he was meant to be there all along.

This first jump, he now knew, would lead to many more. His destiny. With Eros by his side. Forever falling in and out of love. Forever falling. As all gods did, like stars, from the moments of their births.

*

"Love does not dominate, it cultivates" – Goethe

Dear Reader:

Thank you for reading my alternate myth romance.

If you enjoyed this, you might also enjoy subscribing to my newsletter. I put it out about six times a year to announce new books and upcoming projects, and I always have sales and freebies to offer readers both from myself and other authors I enjoy reading. If you subscribe at the link below, you can get a free copy of my book "Letters to an Android".

Happy Reading!

Wendy Rathbone

Contact links for Wendy:

Facebook: https://www.facebook.com/wendy.rathbone.3

Blog: http://wendyrathbone.blogspot.com/

Newsletter sign up (you get a free copy of the critically acclaimed "Letters to an Android"): https://www.instafreebie.com/free/3ErH0

About Wendy Rathbone

I love to write. I have this thing about words and how they are used to describe beauty, love, and all the things that open us up inside to our true self, our power. Words do that for me. They make me happy. The new moon smiling, the sadness of a fallen feather at dusk, predatory eyes gazing through smoke.

The reason I write romance these days is because the overwhelming power of falling in love (which has been proven to heal even cancer) is a game-changer. It makes sad people instantly happy. It makes bleak reality look sun-warmed and friendly again.

I have written in all genres: scifi, fantasy, horror, paranormal, contemporary, erotica, romance. My poetry has won awards, publishing contracts, and was recently nominated for a Pushcart. I am a hybrid writer, publishing both indie (under my press name Eye Scry Designs) and with publishers, most recently with Dreamspinner Press.

I keep coming back to romance. Gay romance. Male/male romance. Maybe it was the wonderful start I got when I was very young in Star Trek slash fanfiction. Something about that stuck. The idea of two men falling in love in a society that has winced at that sort of thing for far too long (when in ancient times and other cultures it is considered normal) is alluring. The forbidden is imminently appealing and erotic to me. Many of my themes involve abduction, pleasure slavery, indentured servitude, imprisonment. It's like, with my writing, I'm constantly breaking out of some self-imposed cage and letting my wings unfurl until I can finally fly.

This is why I write. This is what makes me burn.

All my books are available on Kindle and Createspace. So if you have the urge, go take a look. See what's on the shelf.

Love to you all!

Wendy Rathbone

Ganymede: Abducted by the Gods
Wendy Rathbone

My name is Ganymede, and I have been betrayed.

Every boy my age dreams of leaving home to embark on a noble adventure, but never does any boy imagine it happening as it did to me. On the evening of my 18th naming day, when I expected no more than a chalice of wine and a few drunken flirtations to tempt my innocence, I was instead sold by my father to the god, Zeus - not because of anything particular I had ever done or said, but solely because I am considered beautiful among mortals, and my father found more value in a few gold coins than in the well-being of his youngest son.

To be honest, I never believed in the gods, but my lack of belief held no power in Olympus or on Earth. Now under Zeus's influence, I am kept drunk on ambrosia in the sun-lit halls of the immortals, alternately amazed and horrified at the power these beings hold over others, and how darkly they influence the progress of humanity itself. How very much I want to hate Zeus for kidnapping me, and yet he shows me mostly kindness, even on that fateful night when we shared a bed for the first time. Kindness, yes, but also a godly and unyielding refusal to take no for an answer... probably because he could read my ambrosia-fevered curiosity as much as my naive, inexperienced terror. He owns me, after all, just as he owns everything else, so perhaps it never occurred to him that a captive and a slave might not make the best of lovers.

Throughout my time at Olympus - who's to say how long I've been here, for time on Olympus is not the same as that on Earth - the only thing that gives me hope comes to me in dreams and visions. His name is Sable and he is a magnificent shape-shifter in the form of a giant raven. When he first spoke to me in my mind it was with a resonance unlike any I had ever known - his mind and mine sounding a single note together, a song without words, a promise of freedom, a glimpse of some distant but very real possibility of this thing we humans call Love. But now he is silent. Perhaps I dreamed his voice. Perhaps I have finally lost my mind...

"Fans of *"The Song of Achilles"* by Madeline Miller, and *"Captive Prince"* by C.S. Pacat will especially enjoy Rathbone's version of the Ganymede's myth." – A.J., blog reviewer

PREY
Wendy Rathbone

When the rescued slaves were first brought on board my ship, I saw only the one. The one they called Arcana. And though I realized the others had all suffered similar fates - fearsome torture and erotic conditioning that had estranged them from whoever they had once been - I focused on the one who met my eyes with what could only be interpreted as a defiantly seductive lure, while the others held their gazes downward, at their feet, at the floor, at the past which had shaped them and undoubtedly doomed them to any sort of normal life.

Not so with Arcana. That one had no shame in whatever had happened to him. In that one blinding moment when we saw one another for the first time, I knew he was as brash as he was beautiful, and I knew without any doubt that he had chosen me - though for what dark agenda, I could not have said.

My heart went cold and silent in my chest. My throat was dry. My breathing faltered and I was forever changed.

***

We danced. Captain Mordecai and I. Not any traditional dance, but a dance of power. A battle of yin and yang, light and dark, pleasure and torment. A dangerous dance of right and wrong in a single moment caught outside the tendrils of Time.

It was easy to see the raw and sensual power in that man's gaze. But also the fear. Fear of being seen for who he was behind his carefully-constructed masks. Fear of finally surrendering to the dangerous desires he clearly felt when he looked at me, knowing my past, knowing I had been enslaved by sadistic aliens. Knowing I had not only enjoyed it, but had come to love my master. All the wrong things. So very wrong.

That was when I knew he wanted me. That was when I knew I needed him.

That was when I knew I had him exactly where we both needed him to be.

LETTERS TO AN ANDROID
Wendy Rathbone

Cobalt is a created human, vat grown and born adult, with no human rights and indentured to serve others for the duration of his life. Liyan is a young man with wanderlust in his eyes, embarking on a career that takes him to the furthest regions of space. The two become unlikely friends and create a memorable long-distance correspondence. Through Liyan, Cobalt gets to explore the universe, living vicariously through his friend's wave transmissions. A strong bond develops between them that not even the stars can put asunder.

―――――――――――

Now you know an android who writes poetry.

This is all your fault. Did you not read my last wave telling you extracurricular activities for my kind are discouraged? Of course this is harmless and strangely enjoyable and does not necessarily require me to leave the hotel. Pel would not care if I wrote lines of equations or nonsensical juxtaposed words. As long as the act does not bring my mental state into question.

However, in history, poetry is often written by the rebels.

So we can keep this to ourselves.

Let me know about your lieutenant's test.

And to give you peace of mind, I never believed you observed me as anything other than human.

Some people are and always will be hateful bigots. Most people are simply uncomfortable in speaking to "property." And anyway, friendship, like poetry, is also discouraged.

Your friend,
Cobalt

LACE
Wendy Rathbone

Lace is a being from another dimension on Earth. He cannot die and humans call his kind "vampire" and declare war on them.

Firi is a human military soldier, a trained guard, who has met Lace twice in his young life and formed a bond with him.

In a world where humans and vampires are arch enemies, where vampires are eradicated in horrible ways, where being a vampire-lover means a death sentence, can Firi and Lace ever find each other again and explore the feelings they have for each other?

Will Lace be able escape his government prison, and the amnesia that keeps him from accessing his true powers?

Can Firi, the boy he met in the woods ten years ago, ever hope to help him?

A male/male romance about secrets that can get you killed, impossible rescues, and old lovers who cannot be trusted.

The Foundling
by Wendy Rathbone

Diego is a powerful man with a tragic past. Out on the expansive ocean in his private yacht, he discovers a beautiful and mysterious man adrift on a raft, near death. The bond that forms between them in the aftermath of Alec's rescue is one of fierce passion, though lacking in trust. Can they make it work, or will Alec's amnesia bring forth secrets so disturbing as to tear them apart? A passionately erotic love story of desire and darkness, exquisite and explicit.

I can see his struggle between gratitude and uneasiness. He is buffeted by all things new and strange. He does not know where he is from, who he is or what happened to him. He does not know me. There has not been enough time to transition between strangers and friendship.

This isolation of his is something I can identify with, but it is also a feeling no one can help him with until or unless he gets his own life back. And his memory.

If that doesn't happen, then it will take time for him to build a new life. He is polite to me, even friendly, but even a night together during a storm with his arms wrapped tight around my waist doesn't calm the surge I see inside him, the emptiness, the loss, possibly even panic. That night may have reinforced some trust in me, but so far not enough for him to completely relax.

He seeks me out, though. That's something. He sits by me at dinner when he can have any seat of his choosing. I watch him closely when he does not realize it. At dinner the following night after we had only 'slept' together, and before we go to bed again in separate rooms, I notice everything about him, how he moves, the way the air warms when he is closer to me, the dry sheen of his lips as they part for more air when he is reacting to something, or speaking, or eating.

His hands still shake. Anyone else might not notice because he keeps them clasped into fists at his sides or, while sitting, pressed tight to his lap.

I spend another fretful night alone. I dream restlessly, wild, loud and colorful visions I cannot recall at all as soon as my eyes open. All I know is the dreams leave me unfulfilled, impatient.

SONS OF NEVERLAND
by Della Van Hise

"The virtuosity shown here is only the beginning of a pyrotechnic talent unfolding into the hidden dimensions of the human and nonhuman spirit."
-Jacqueline Lichtenberg

Set against a backdrop of contemporary culture, *Sons of Neverland* explores the universal questions of love, sex and death - the three most crucial challenges every human being must face. Stefan London is a grieving man, suffering through the loss of his young daughter. When he goes to a science fiction convention in the hopes of meeting her friends, he encounters instead a young man who is dangerously seductive and undeniably magical. Lured into the night, Stefan soon discovers himself in a place where vampires are real, and the world is not at all what he has always believed, and immortality is only a deep red kiss away.

But the price of eternal life is high, and as his handsome maker warns, "Through my blood you will learn a secret which will compel you to live forever, yet a secret so sinister it will haunt you for that same eternity."

The secret will haunt you, too.

———

"This book zones on the question of immortality. However, this is not just the decadent historical immortality of the long-lived vampire, it is immortality as a change in one's perception. This is the story behind the story, delivered by characters that are hyper-real - each one loaded with symbolism. *Sons of Neverland* will have you filled, even brimming over with the sense of Mysterium Tremendum et Fascinans. Go there for a full helping of the numinous." (A Reviewer on Amazon)

Prince of Umberlight
Alexis Fegan Black

"If Prince of Umberlight doesn't rattle your cage, you're more dead than the undead!" **-Night Readers**

Thorn may be an 800 year old vampire, but he does not possess the ability to create others of his kind, and so he is cursed to fall in love with mortals, only to watch them grow old and die. Torn by grief, Thorn denounces his immortality and enters into a comatose oblivion for decades.

When he awakens, he is no longer in London, but finds himself in a world spun into being by his own desires - a world where Time and Death do not exist, a world where it is forever autumn, where the Parish of Shadows and the River of Stars become his home. It is in this world of Umberlight that he meets Atom - an interloper into his private sanctuary, but also an impudent imp who is destined to reveal to Thorn the three dangerous elements a vampire must possess in order to become a Creator.

The Art of Brutality.
Submission to Dark Desire.
Love.

YEAR OF THE RAM
Della Van Hise

Year of the Ram was described by one reviewer as... "A space-faring male/male romance full of love, angst, and longing."

Only after Star Commander Morgan Diego becomes an exile as a result of a Galaxy Corps political blunder does he begin to realize how much he valued the companionship of his second in command - the mysterious Lucien, an Alfarian who is more elven than human, with peculiar powers & abilities which begin to unfold as he, too, realizes what he has lost.

Separated by circumstance from his former life, Morgan is thrust into a world where he must survive by his wits. When he meets a peculiar little old man calling himself Kim Le, Morgan finds himself in a situation where he is required to master The Art - not only a form of human & extraterrestrial martial arts, but a way of living and being that will alter his life forever.

At the temple, he is introduced to his new teacher, another Alfarian who begins to steal his heart - a heart which is already promised to Lucien. Torn and conflicted, Morgan struggles with the world he left behind and the world he now inhabits.

Beginning to believe he may never again return to his ship and to the friends and loved ones he left behind, he is all the more frustrated and heartbroken when a new Master arrives at the temple: a man to whom Morgan is immediately drawn both mentally and physically, a man who is strikingly familiar... yet utterly alien.

Year of the Ram is a fully-fleshed novel, approximately 97000 words, with a focus on the love story and romance angle. Set against a science fiction milieu, it explores the infinite possibilities of the human and alien heart. Sexual content is explicit, though is not the primary focus of the novel.

For those who like a romance that forces its characters to contemplate the ecstasies and the agonies of love... you will enjoy *Year of the Ram.*

All of our titles are available directly from our website, on Amazon, or may be ordered from most booksellers. Thanks for reading us!

Eye Scry Publications
A Visionary Publishing Company
www.eyescrypublications.com